Weirdtongue

A Glistenberry Romance

D. F. Lewis

InkerMen Press
2010

Weirdtongue: A Glistenberry Romance

by
D. F. Lewis

Copyright © D. F. Lewis 2010
This edition copyright © InkerMen Press 2010

Cover Pictures © D. F. Lewis 2010

InkerMen Press
Ashby-de-la-Zouch
info@inkermenpress.co.uk
www.inkermenpress.co.uk

This is a work of fiction.

978-0-9562749-4-6

British Library Cataloguing in Publication Data

Lewis, D. F. (Des. F.), 1948-
   Weirdtongue : a Glistenberry romance.
   1. Horror tales.
   I. Title
   823.9'14-dc22

ISBN-13: 9780956274946

Weirdtongue

D F LEWIS

'I come here,' the Weirdmonger roared, *'to sell Weirds, and Weirds are merely Words that materialize into all sorts of true existence the moment I release them from between my lips…'*

Even these introductories squawked into the sky like forgotten memories of what it was like before one was born.

Weirdmonger

A
VISIT TO THE
NARRATIVE HOSPITAL

Today I lick porridge from a bowl, mapped with jammy smears.

Forgotten memories of what it was like before one was born? I tried to give myself time to absorb the implications brought by the visitor to my hospital ward. A visitor (he said) with wide visibilities of Summerset from a tower on a hill, with the animal zodiac embedded in the fields and hills below. The vanishing sun (he said) silted, rather than lowered, into the broken horizon.

The Weirdmonger never had a name. He was the original nemophile. I had read of his doings. So far only one scribe had dared mention his existence. One scribe, one character. He told me by the end of his visit I would learn his true name. A historic moment. When a scribe's away, the scribe's creations do play, they say. Or at least the Weirdmonger said, and that at least made it true enough for me to remember it as once being true even before he said it.

'Hey,' I suddenly said, 'who are you?'

A nurse looked askance from the other side of the room, presumably at my raised voice. She had been told that the Weirdmonger was a close relative of mine. And I had not gainsaid this. Too late now. I looked appealingly towards her, hoping she would come over to double-check the relative identities of our two dark shapes sitting in the visitors' alcove near the makeshift library. The nurse called this alcove a carrel. A private study-cubicle. I wasn't sure. But I had seen many inmates entertaining visitors in this carrel over the years. This was my first time. I was rarely graced with visitors; I had called myself unlucky, bereft.

Now, I wasn't so sure. Visitors came in several disguises, some lighter than others. And this one today was not exactly an imponderable, but an undesirable.

Many years before, I had spotted a certain visitor being entertained by another inmate; I felt sure it was not that inmate's visitor by rights because the visitor resembled my mother. A woman had looked plaintively over at me but left without visiting me. So, indeed, I knew she had visited someone whom she had not recognised at all. Brings tears to my eyes, even today.

During the posy of pauses encouraged by my thoughts, the Weirdmonger had idly picked up a loose book from the carrel table and riffled through it.

'Why are you here?' he said, looking up, instinctively aware that my mind was now empty.

'I have trouble distinguishing between being ill and being well,' I answered. There was a medical name for this condition, but it didn't fit. I was never cold. In fact I suffered from the heat.

The sun was baking through the window even now as I watched tussocks being hustled by a dry wind.

'My own trouble is distinguishing between present and past,' he countered, with a glinting look of boastful waywardness.

I see him clearly. He has all the features that one associates with yesterday.

The nurse plucks my fingers from the bowl of book, teasing the letters n-e-m-o-p-h-i-l-e[1] back upon the slowly reconstituting leaves and then leaving them outside to dry into w-e-i-r-d-t-o-n-g-u-e. The frontispiece was never discovered as I had swallowed it. They always said I had swallowed the dictionary. Wordiness and worry, those were my fate. Maybe that was the cause of my ambivalent health. A mixed blessing, if being full of words meant one could

---

[1] Nemo = Latin for 'nobody'

dream with the requisite words to describe that one was empty of them.

At least I found the visitor's name on the spine that I never attempted to eat, though it did show gnaw-marks. The nurse tried to hide it. Mummerset. Mummerset was the name. Gregory Mummerset. The name rung up all sorts of futures and pasts, without which this gift of the present would never have been granted. The ward had many inmates that were ever changing their minds. A hospital is made of many wards. We exchanged visiting cards cut from other spines. Then we tore them up.

Through the ward window could be spotted the back-end of the Weirdmonger's medicine wagon that, as well as trundling away into the slow setting, also created it, brought it gradually into existence.

∞

Gregory was officially cured and excused further in-patient treatment, soon realising—as he did by virtue of the cure and his renewed powers of realisation—that part of the treatment he had just undergone in the hospital ward was the disease itself. Nemophilia had been induced to remove any taint of nemophobia (a variant form of self-mythology). Indeed, this inducing of nemophilia—allowing vacuous urges to be released from their pent-up mind-trap by the hare-chase of aspirational non-existence—revealed aspects of an extreme nemophobia (self-centeredness where everything was self and nothing non-self), this being his more natural state of existence when unaffected by disease and this state of being unaffected by disease, paradoxically, was the same disease in disguise.

In summary, Nemophilia was the desire to be a nobody, but not simply a desire, but an intractable passion to self-efface or to become both nameless and unnameable.

Nemophobia was its apparent opposite by hating that nemophiliac self.

In this way, nemophobia and nemophilia, whilst superficial opposites, were also part of a synergistic, symbiotic oxymoron-relationship, a situation that encouraged further self-effacement by needing to face up to the self-disgust created by the recognition of the self itself. It also created extreme wordiness of expression as a by-product: i.e. an unwanted side effect.

Meanwhile, the quality (or not) of the self itself did not matter; it was simply the very recognition of it (of *any* self) that created this paradoxical disease (akin but distinct from Dream Sickness, of which more later).

His eyes skimmed the hospital release papers as he gradually recognised the surroundings of his own flat, still dishevelled from his absence, but about to be further dishevelled by his presence. The name 'Gregory Mummerset' was clearly printed at the top together with his real-world address (this flat). Followed by scrawled officialese, presumably a prescription for his General Practitioner or his pharmacist. Gregory did not need to know. He cringed at knowing his own name. He'd rather be called the Weirdmonger. At least *that* name did not exist as a signpost for a real person.

There came a knocking at his door. He had been left here only an hour before by the hospital car. And the driver had knocked upon leaving in the way Gregory imagined he had been taught to do, as a dress rehearsal for the real knocking that now had indeed arrived. Gregory did not believe in ghosts. But he was yet unaware of the power of fiction to produce them in real life. He was soon to learn many things as he was taken abroad on a Grand Tour to all the health spas of Middle Europe. Indeed to the Magic Mountain itself.

He lifted himself heavily from the table-seat (reminding him of the one in the carrel at the hospital)—and opened the door.

'Hiya, Gregory,' said the beaming face of his girl friend. She was soon remembered and Gregory gave her a light kiss on the cheek.

'How are you, Suzie?' he said. 'I didn't have chance to let you know that I was coming home today.'

'I somehow knew, when I saw the curtains drawn,' she said.

He looked over her shoulder as if he expected someone to be behind her.

'Why didn't you visit me?'

She shrugged. 'Mum has been ill. My hands have been full. Sorry.'

'I only had one visitor and that was yesterday.'

'You've only been in three days.'

'It seemed like years.'

'Are you feeling better?'

Gregory frowned. He did not know. Part of his bad health was not being able to differentiate good and bad health. 'I must be better. Do I look better?'

'You look great. Aren't you going to let me in?'

'I've got nothing in,' he said looking back into the room. 'Are you alone?'

'Of course, I'm alone,' she said, taking it upon herself to cross the threshold, ignoring the half-hearted attempts to guard his territory against visitors.

Her shadow—at cross-purposes with the direction of the light—followed her in.

∞

Gregory Mummerset was once a boy. He was from a poor family. Or he was *told* they were poor to excuse or explain the type of clothes worn, the meagre food and lack of television.

'But TV wasn't invented then,' he thought, as if arguing with those who had somehow taken charge of his past.

He was, however, fully in control of his boyhood dreams. Nobody could intervene upon *them*. Meanwhile, those who wanted to intervene did intervene in respect of the actuality of his boyhood days themselves. Telling was interference.

He remembered—without fear of such interference—two recurring boyhood dreams in particular, dreams haunting that ancient sleep of his.

The first figured a credibly sized modern mobile phone (long before these things were invented) with a circular dial that most real old-fashioned black bakelite telephones boasted in those days. The sprung holes, however, in the tiny dial were impossible for normal sized fingers to push round, even a child's.

The second dream was more difficult to describe, if not remember. Gregory could do with some interference to establish the full feel or contents of the dream. But he eschewed it. He required his dreams untouched by *any* hand, let alone a writer's. He dreamed he was a woman of mature years and unbecoming looks, the wife of a man in charge of a race similar to a flat horse race from springable stalls or (to fit the era in which the dream happened within his then contemporary sleep) more like greyhounds in traps ready to catapult after the mock clockwork hare, ripening itself for the mad spin round the track. Yet the animals in *this* race appeared to be sizeable cattle of a strange rumination—and they were lowing in expectation of their own race, as he (or she) inferred. It was dark in the hall outside the ponderously-punctuated-by-the-sound-of-a-clock-ticking parlour where the dreamer was with her baby tuckoo. The moocows were readily pent-up by inferred stalls as evidenced by their crumpled horns and awkward demeanour ... about to race along the even darker single-file steepness that vanished upwards like stairs in a small terraced house. They kept twirling their mobile faces upon the spectator at the open parlour door. But what was the delay? A certain dread at even questioning it. The dreamer's husband was obviously having problems releasing the cattle because they started to turn ugly in tantrums of sluggish impatience. The dreamer abruptly slammed the parlour door in a panic which she failed to comprehend. A mother's instinct to safeguard her baby tuckoo? And then she began to feel a deep pressure behind the shut door, gradually deepening further, visibly straining the lock and her ability to push back against it beyond reason. At that point, Gregory's dream always ended when simpler, yet unreportable, words took over. And maybe the dreamer continued, whilst Gregory woke. Or Gregory truly became a permanent dreamer in a dream world, leaving a different boy to wake. Or he was baby tuckoo itself, aware of the dream by being *in* the dream. Inference or interference, which of these it was, remained clouded. Even today there are no mobiles in dreams.

∞

Blasphemy Fitzworth was, as many already knew, a cat's meat man who sold his wares throughout the winding catacombs of streets in Victorian London. The children that followed in the wake of his steaming, bubble-sounding meatcart (as he pushed—or more often pulled—its tiny sprung wheels) were often cock-a-hoop with life, despite the mouching, slouching way of dirt and life that threaded their young bones with yellow marrowfat as well as feeding further redless pigments into their bloodcourses. They joyfully shouted 'Feemy' (a foreshortening of his name) when they heard his costermonger's cry in an indeterminate distance, slowly drawing nearer and nearer from seemingly impossible angles of approach:

'Gout cat! Spout cat! Watch their whiskers sprout, cat!'

The legend—not among the kids as they were too young to know—indicated that Feemy Fitzworth was a spy from other times, from other worlds alternating with ours, ever on the search for evidence of greater and (then again) greater Gods than those in which the indigenous peoples already believed. A step-ladder toward the noumenon. Ecumenical, if not economical, with the truth.

The choice of cat's meat vending as a disguise was first described by another visitor to our times, but facts got so crosswired (not only the times whence this scribe came but even his identity and whereabouts themselves) that they have become ludicrously confused with where he was going or whence he'd just been and why. Some even believed that the scribe was Feemy himself. But *that* confusion was one confusion too far. A first straw that broke the linear dromedary's back. But none knew. None probably cared.

Chelly Mildeyes was one such kid, maybe a kid in disguise, who followed Feemy, a spy upon another spy or, more likely, a reminder of the ghost she replaced. But that is only hearsay. Other texts may tell fresher truths, but today we can only be sufficed with this one, given any timely exegesis by external sources or not. She certainly mixed in with the other scrawny, tornly dressed kids with a will and a believability that makes any doubt quite parsimonious and self-demeaning.

She plumped a fist into the meatcart's back pan, evidently not eager to clutch at the valves of still heart-beating brisket melts (hence the fist rather than a clawing open palm), but to see if she could do it without Feemy noticing. A devilment for its own sake. Either to enhance her disguise in face of Feemy's own disguise or, more likely, because she actually enjoyed devilment for its own sake. She was soon interfered from her childish dipping by the sight of Feemy saluting the sun as a sort of shading of the eyes against its glare. She thought he said he could see Great Old Ones gliding in with huge cattle faces from a direction he'd not expected. Their lowing filled the sky with a monotonous low-key invisible thunderstorm.

It was then he heard his mobile ring—out-trilling the squeaking meat of the middle pan where he'd stowed it.

∞

'Want some tea?'

Suzie made herself at home, whilst Gregory relearned the art of making the tea he had just offered.

'Hadn't you better ring her?' she said, idly looking through the parlour window at the empty street.

'Ring who?' came the voice from the kitchen.

Suzie scratched the back of her neck. 'Scat!' she said absentmindedly—more to herself than anything else. 'Your Mum … to tell her that you're out of hospital.'

'Oh … yes, I suppose I'd better. Not that she ever cared about me. She never visited. But you say I was only in for three days? Hmmm. But I don't know her number since she moved.'

'Try her mobile. She won't have changed that. She's had the same mobile through six husbands!' Suzie laughed. 'Anyway, how are you really? Got rid of the gremlins?'

The word 'gremlins' was a euphemism for Dream Sickness, a plague of which had only recently been taken under control by the authorities. The difficulty was to trust that the doctors weren't under its influence themselves because different forms of the complaint would have caused them to practice equally different methods of treating it. Now the plague was effectively under control, indeed almost one hundred per cent eradicated, anyone claiming to be suffering from it was immediately branded a malingerer or simply work-shy. Gregory was one of the very last patients credited with the validity of the sickness. In various forms, it had different names, most of which Gregory had now forgotten or been forced to forget as part of the treatment. It was still unclear if any form of the sickness was indeed just another way of saying it was a perception of it by someone was also suffering from it (or not). The names were merely labels of convenience whatever the setting. Once one started studying these factors and sorting them out into the correct pigeon-holes, the hazier became the task itself that had started so clearly. Even writing about these factors at all made them worse. One started with a clear mind—but such clarity laid bare the implications of the sickness which in turn radiated back to the clear mind that one tried to remember as the one you had started off with before commencing the analysis with a subsequent confident hope of future synthesis ... thus making even the earlier conversation about tea, mobiles and mothers just a misty memory from another world.

Gregory picked up the phone and dialled the number he found in a notebook as being for his Mum's mobile. A man's voice answered: 'Yes?' There was a background noise of children shouting in play.

'Is Mum there?'

Suzie stared meaninglessly upon the tea's meniscus as if scrying it for omens, whilst Gregory held the phone away from his ear: his turn for staring ... in disbelief. The clatter of wooden wheels outside the house filled the empty hot street with a sign of the Weirdmonger's return. A wind-ballooning canvas-zeppelin marked with signs of a circus... followed by a troop of clowns dressed in advertising sandwich-boards each bearing a single truth.

Suzie shrugged off what was hugging her like a winter coat.

Gregory, in turn, shook his head as he emerged from his own misty memory. He stared at Suzie. 'Yes, I'd better ring my Mum. She may have my bank book.'

∞

The City of London, well beyond its Victorian allotment in time, suffered the blitz from wartime bombers, lighting up

A Glistenberry Romance

St Paul's Cathedral from ground beacons poking the sky with spot-tunnels of light and the crepitations interpenetrating such stained-glass-window-filtered shafts of Godness by means of smoke and fire. This was nineteen forty something—not even the narrator responsible for this tranche of fiction or reality being able to plump on the exact date, for fear of triggering unwelcome repercussions further along the time-line (back or forward). The river sounded far too close for this to be a sane London geography.

Padgett Weggs, a dosser who squatted within cardboard bedding quite close to the Cathedral, watched the sky in awe. The old-fashioned bomb-doors slipped their greyhounds of the night for racing against the suicide versions that rained in from the future. Slots of darker night opened up above Padgett; he both feared and loved these slots: fear, since fear was not voluntary; love, since love of his own ease of death would remove him from lovelessness and famine.

He saw more than he wanted to see. He was writing a book in his head. It was either a real book. Or a dream of a book. Evacuee children with labelled suitcases carried books in their heads when they travelled miles, along railtracks, from their family towards no greater retrospective safety in the countryside. Because one day the books themselves would explode more devastatingly than the blitz bombs.

Padgett's book described Gregory Mummerset. A moon-faced man with a beard and glasses, mole on the left cheek. Quite a nice gentleman who had given his name to the Weirdmonger. Padgett needed to read till the end to prove or disprove that the Weirdmonger and Gregory were the same individual, if not the same body. Gregory was out of his depth. The things in his head made the skull feel bigger. He was getting older without having fully planned for death. It was as if life itself expunged death with a brainwash of busy projects and a false claim for fame. Fame was never immortality. He must have known, surely. His intermittent wife Suzie was just another shadow in a coat, even on hot summer's days when the tussocks were hustled by a dry wind. At times, his mind, if not he himself, settled at the top of Glastonbury Tor watching the evacuee children arriving for their wartime billets. He made out a bit of the animal zodiac in the fields and hills around. Torus. He wondered if he was a child who would never find his mother again, even when computers later were to allow universal communication and searching into the deepest corners of memory and lost heritage. Blitzed search-engines of food-for-thought to be used as firewalls or screensavers: far preferable to the cheap-cut spam these evacuee children would be faced with tonight.

The book also described Feemy Fitzworth as a story within a story. Feemy left the City and Victorian times in general and reached the coast where a harbour drifted into gossamer twilights, rather than the twilights coming to the harbour. He was due to take a voyage for the spice-trails in far off Cathay and Samarkand. Better than selling his version of cat's meat spam. He missed Chelly, but all the children (including Chelly herself) had vanished towards forgotten times in which it became unsafe to be born at all. Evacuated from history itself. Feemy's face was lined. He was a rather stout person who enjoyed being jolly and noisy. Yet he loved the quiet interludes of fantasy that he was about to enjoy. Given the book's ability to follow him there.

Padgett was fighting on more than one fiction front. It remained to be seen whether the nemonities between each front could summon up their sinews of reality. He lost the thread temporarily as a particularly loud firestorm erupted in spasmodically deliberate trials at creating the blitz bomb that would cause it. The Cathedral reddened in pain and grew dark again. He heard the river drawing ever closer, threatening to make the Cathedral a straddling one. He went back to his book, unfolding the corner of the page he had folded down inside his head.

∞

Measured out in words. He paced down the street outside the block of flats, leaving Suzie posted at the window of his kitchen to watch him test out a theory. That the canvas wagon they had seen passing was much bigger than even a huge circus tent, judging by the scale and perspective he was now rhythmically intoning under his breath from the water hydrant to the postbox.

And if this fact were proved, it would also prove that Gregory was still suffering from Dream Sickness and, not only him, Suzie, too.

∞

Feemy Fitzworth watched the departing coast slowly vanish into yet another mist of memory.

The shanty-singing sailors were already getting into the swing of things, as the sails bellied out with a wind that belied that very mist.

The horizon, however, soon glowed with an orange worm wriggling along it—and the towers of a city that punctuated it like striated windfarms. The journey had been foreshortened towards this new coast. So much so that narration itself had taken a backseat, suffering its own form of writerly sickness more akin to blockage than dreaming. Continents of imagination diminished to a pinprick.

∞

Weggs slowly unpeeled himself from the damp cardboard; dampened not only by the city's gritty dew but also by his own liquefying incontinence.

London was waking to a blanket beige calm creeping up the sky as a forerunner of a timeless sun.

Ruins steamed, rather than smoked, in the rising heat. Time to regroup, before the next onslaught.

The dome of the Cathedral quickly bared itself of bovine Irreducibles, because, in any sane universe, they could only clamber there out of daylight hours. This dome: the Tor of his dreams inverted into a stone plateau that belied curved geometry except when one imagined it for real.

A crocodile of modern schoolchildren in Indian File, all with labelled satchels on their shoulders, momentarily ghosted past along Ludgate Hill on an imputed outing to see the inside of the wartime Cathedral.

∞

The Weirdmonger sat in his medicine wagon, hatching more Weirds in the guise of Words. Nearby he heard the clowns—working beyond their own union's demarcation lines of duty—pulling the guy-ropes of the canvas Big Top, with groans as well as the sea-songs they had learnt from musical dreams. Varicoloured smears dripped up their faces like tears returning to mascara. One clown in particular—unseen, yet thought of, by the Weirdmonger—plotted to punish any ringmaster who might throw custard pies at him that very night. He left one guy-rope over-loosened and a top pinion awkwardly sited within the rope's purview of leverage.

Meanwhile, the Weirdmonger left his wagon—himself unseen—to resume hospital visiting for replacement ringmasters. Too many had escaped, during the current plagues, so an ever-renewable source was paramount. So much so, the paying audiences themselves became depleted. A vicious circle that even the Weirdmonger had failed to address.

∞

The library was unusually silent as a pair of disembodied hands sorted various papers into the pigeon-holes of the carrel's wooden face-facing wall. A writer who was lonely and did not benefit from the company of his own characters in the same way as these characters benefited from each other. They were firm and fast friends, these characters, when off duty, despite the lack of focussed delineation so far in being able to pick them out from any old crowd.

Hence, the need to sort names with personalities and then with physical features by means of the current collating in the abandoned library. Hence, too, the empty shadow—known as nemophilia—welling across him like a blanket mindset of inarticulate ink.

∞

The sailors lowered their sails. The ship managed the rest of the long voyage into the harbour by means of a motorised force that was hidden from view. Its noise was gutturally similar to half-articulate human speech. Complete with glottal stops. Feemy Fitzworth watched great flagons of thick black fluid being fed into various openings in the deck, as imputed fuel. Taking him—by means of crudely engineered mechanisms of motive force as lubricated by the flesh of those who worked in the bowels of the ship—from one mist of memory to another. He remembered the stuff he used to sell from his meatcart, liquidised black-pudding, similar to the fuel in consistency, in look and, possibly, in feel, if not in edibility.

Feemy had only met the Captain the day before, but by that reckoning, based on memory of duration, the meeting must have been before the voyage started. Or, even, whilst it was still being planned.

The Captain told him that it may be Victorian in London, but the rest of the world would likely never to have heard of the Queen who had given the era its name.

The Captain was the tallest member of the crew but surely that feature wasn't the only qualification for his position in the ranks of navigation. Yet he was the only one who could reach the handle of the door to the wheel room.

As they eye-balled each other over the dinner table in the Captain's quarters, the conversation became flippant and casual, rather than the earlier seriousness concerning latitudes, sextants and galley-slaves.

'Where we're going they speak a language called Weirdtongue,' the Captain said, nibbling on some slimy provender Feemy himself had contributed to the ship's victuals. Fishily slimy, despite being meat.

'Oh? Do they have people to translate? I thought they spoke Chinese where we were going,' said Feemy.

'We changed tack halfway through the voyage. The cargo was moved halfway across the world so that we could pick it up to return it.'

Feemy looked quizzical. Little Chelly would have enjoyed this small talk. Ludicrous as some of it was.

Feemy missed his small customers in the City streets around St Paul's and wondered how he had reached this particular pass in life. A drug-runner was never a job he was ambitious about as a boy. He'd rather have been a train-driver. He scratched his head. Not only was the conversation hitting double-notes of misfired music in the meaning, so were his own thoughts.

'Can you speak Weirdtongue?'

The Captain shook his head up and down and then from side to side, as if the very question was in a language he didn't understand.

∞

Gregory and Suzie decided to celebrate his first day out in the world after hospital by going to the circus. This had been a childhood pleasure as a child. And conveniently a new circus had just hit town, as advertised by the tilting airship over the park—where the big tent had been erected and surrounded by a congeries of caravans. And a menagerie of lows, roars, yaps and squeaks.

They left the flat and headed towards the park via his Mum's place where he reclaimed the bank book he'd previously left in her safekeeping. She hardly said a word. In fact, she may not have been there at all, and Gregory possibly helped himself by using the front-door key that was kept in the porch under the slipmat.

They first visited a smaller tent with a board saying 'Friques', a sideshow beside the main attraction. This contained many creaturely curios that had been collected around the world, living, breathing, usually silent. One enclosure contained a creature so far into its own death, it must have been there and come back again, by the look of it, because it was extruding a substance that had become itself: a substance that was nothing any creature could have produced short of having died and become its own excrement with, in turn, its own excrement, i.e. an excrement's excrement quite fouler than its origination covered by an effigy-skin of itself to make recognition possible. Padgett Weggs, however, did not recognise it was himself. For one thing, there was no mirror in the enclosure.

Usually in such shows, one is not allowed to talk to the exhibits. Suzie was quite aghast at the sight of this thing but soon realised it was the remnant of a war veteran, someone who had helped fight fires during the blitz, before being dossed out into modern times. Or so the poor blighter claimed through a series of glottal stops. It was always good to listen to the stories of old-timers, turgid in tone and register though they may have been. Humouring old-timers was an art in itself. Reliving their highs and lows of life.

Weirdtongue

Encouraging them to prattle on about this, that and the other. Learning, where you were able to do so, about aspects of life that were dying out with the people who had lived them for real rather than fictionally. While Suzie held this conversation with living history, Gregory left the stifling tent for a breather outside.

The park was a strange one and shimmered in the heat. So hot this summer, the grass had yellowed over and the distant church spire—beyond the boating-lake—was a reminder of times beyond reality. That was what heat could do. Make things tenuous. Less simple to understand. Almost providing a protection against the dark implications of transgressed time. Proustian, without the necessity of understanding what the word meant.

The airship was a mere speck on the horizon now, where the gasworks squatted—obviously to land elsewhere in the conurbation. The Big Top was just opening its doors, if tent-flaps could be credited with such a description. A beady eye in one of the nearby caravans followed Gregory as he prepared to fetch Suzie from amongst the 'Friques'. She liked somersaults. And tonight there would be acrobats, as well as clowns. And a ringmaster with a whip for the circling performers on hooves and claws and slimy long bellies.

∞

Suzie wanted Gregory to return to the 'Friques' sideshow for a quick look at another exhibit. The main circus was not due to start for about thirty minutes, but he found himself reluctant to take unnecessary risks. Life was never risk-free, however, so one needed to create a balance between fear and fortitude.

He had not sensed being watched. So, the next moment, after the arbitrary tabulation, he was relatively relaxed as Suzie took him by the hand towards a very tall figure labelled 'Captain Bintiff'. This evident once-man was stridently garbed in wolfwhistle leathers. He managed to talk despite the interference from a tongue that appeared side-eroded by a rather tough proposition in sherbet dips or acid drops. Shaggily overthick ... protuberant despite signs of premature docking. Stunted, indeed, from further growth by a symbiotic merging with a gum disorder that stretched—with such disorder's own seeming volition—from its normal hidden lairs of disease where brown sockets hardly held the stained teeth in place for talking let alone for eating ... stretched, indeed, to infect vulnerable tissues of the tongue. A tongue hinged by decorative rivets of icy steel. Tipped with a needle from an old-fashioned wind-up gramophone to prevent erosion at least in this business end of the organ as well as to be wielded as a particularly nasty device in the act of love-making. Not that Gregory could imagine anyone willing to submit to such advances.

'Why have your brought me to see this thing?' Gregory asked Suzie. He failed to pay attention to her reply because of Captain Bintiff's simultaneously louder articulations of mislanguage. Gregory had just remembered the hospital's promise of a Grand Tour of Middle European health spas, including the famed Magic Mountain retreat in one of the more forgettably estranged countries that used to be part of the USSR. He looked at his bank book to see if it could bear any extraneous expenses not covered by the National Health Service. He never found it strange how his mind could so easily be diverted from interesting events to more mundane matters. It seemed all part of the parcel of his condition. He was shocked to find the account fleeced. And all his loose change having just been used for getting into 'Friques'. No chance of a circus visit now.

He and Suzie tracked through the gloomier parts of the park, the sun finally silting into the broken horizon at the edge of the city where waste ground predominated and memories began regrouping in gaseous mists over marshland. Then a welling edge of moon grew to a gibbous horn double-tongued by the duty light-fairy blowing all manner of silent music in the shape of illuminations in the northern sky. They listened to the distant Circus fanfare of braying brass as it announced giant snails about to creep sluggishly around in strict formation amid silver-sarabands of glisten without any need of a ringmaster's fire-tipped whips to spur further onward purpose beneath their slimy soles. An attractive trapeze-artist in a thong fell to her fate amid a shelob-spider's safety-net of a web. Gregory knew all this because of the nemonities permeating the sticky summer night air with consciously air-borne fluff-balls of forgotten knowledge. However, some forgotten knowledge was so forgotten it probably was never remembered by anyone, in that there was a single shadow following them quite divorced from their own two moon-forced shadows. Maybe a hybrid of all three.

∞

The bottom fell out of the market. Feemy Fitzworth—originally fresh-faced with hope in a new career overseas—was now crestfallen, faced with a ship that had abandoned him in a place that could only talk a language called Weirdtongue and an indigenous people who could barely speak any language at all. He could recall the ship vanishing into its own new created distance, its tall captain waving from the wheel bridge, and Feemy left with no resources other than buying a cart and selling meat for cats to whomsoever he could find. Two problems: no money to buy a cart and no cats.

What was more, he was no longer effectively 'Overseas' as such, now being on *this* side of the seas. Where he'd come from was now Overseas. Overseas was a moving feast of geographical sense-patterns. Neither sane or insane. Just a fact. And any ambitions for adventures and a new start in the 'Overseas' thus took on a more parochial turn for fat-licking Feemy and left no attractions for this once keen and jolly inhabitant of life.

∞

After crossing the ambient park on that memorable nightwalk back to my flat near the marshland part of the city, a light petting session between Suzie and I ensued without further thought of tongues or snails, the first session for however long I had been in hospital. Yet, before this, something has not yet been reported as far as I can see; Suzie and I had inadvertently seen another 'Frique' which probably both of us regretted seeing, particularly because, one day, we vowed to be parents if we could ever adjust our weight in the scales of petting. Petting above our weight was never something to be taken lightly.

The exhibit was sign-posted 'Tuckoo' and evidently a baby version of this so-named creature, if not the only version possible, with its adulthood stunted at growth. It had a rubber eraser for a head … and so that's the end of that. Nipped in the bud. It was always thus unless I could recover my own non-singularity as an information source.

∞

Padgett Weggs saw the end of the war. He vanished from the St Paul's Cathedral area and tried to make a living from dossing in the Clockhouse Estate of Coulsdon, which was in a sort of no man's land between London and the Surrey Badlands. He had dreams—which he put down to—well, what else could you call it?—dreaming. No one had diagnosed Dream Sickness then, let alone Nemophilia.

One dream was particularly vivid and was sufficiently vivid to make it appear to be a dream of a single dream that he only dreamed once—whilst, effectively, it was a recurring dream over several years. He was an exhibit in a Freak Show that masqueraded as a novella; and, furthermore, he was not just a cipher nor simply a cardboard character in this 'novella'. He was, indeed, destined to be a major protagonist in far-reaching events that several people controlled but controlled only partially in each case. His problem—until he is next given treatment—was fighting against the substance that was both created on his behalf alternately as sustenance and effluence for and from his body but eventually both becoming (as substance) his body itself, without any emotional septic-tank or stand-by Irreducibles to take or milk the strain.

∞

Gregory stared at Suzie—and at their respective mothers who had separately and independently interfered by visiting during the couple's first session of light petting on return from the park, both circus and friques forgotten or at least pushed to the back of the mind where any dream sickness sucked but could not stick.

Suzie's Mum had been ill whilst Gregory had been in hospital. A traditional homely illness like flew or migraine. She was now on the mend and had arrived at Gregory's flat concerned that he we was about to renew his 'evil influence' on her daughter. The bloke's weird, she thought. And Gregory simply knew she thought this so there was not much love lost between them. With many episodes of *Lost* lost, too, with no TV available in the hospital, he couldn't help thinking, with a wry smile.

Gregory's Mum loved Gregory, hence her many failed attempts at visiting him (and no-one else) during hospital visiting hours. Currently, with any dream sickness relatively subdued, both had forgotten the baleful glances between each other as she visited other patients in the visiting carrel, patients she had pretended to be the real Gregory. Equally, mundane matters resumed their importance in day-to-day life with no possible escape into fantasy, real or otherwise. There was a difference between known fantasy and fantasy disguised as reality. But, now, such whimsical concerns—inevitably raising their heads from time to time as they still did—had no option but to retract into their snail-shells, impatiently awaiting the return of any signs of dream sickness or, better still, nemophilia / nemophobia in the minds that controlled such intrinsically uncertain demarcation-lines between (i) reality, (ii) fantasy and (iii) reality/fantasy combined, whilst changing perceptions confused any such ambitions by often being in danger of seeing the actual definitions of (i), (ii) and (iii) as each other's definition.

In consequence (but with no logical connection to enforce any consequence at all between what went before and what followed), Gregory's Mum, showed delight in having rediscovered her son (in company with Suzie whom she quite liked despite disliking her mother who was also present). Despite this, Gregory noticed that his mother kept looking at her mobile, no doubt for text messages from her current 'bloke'.

'Why has my bank book been emptied, Mum?' Gregory suddenly asked, with a look towards Suzie, as if eye-balling his own mother was not possible whatever the provocation.

Suzie's mother looked embarrassed and made as if to depart.

Gregory's Mum looked up from her mobile which had trilled to indicate the arrival of a message.

'It says that he wants more money sent overseas so that he can buy another cart,' she said quite innocently, as if changing the subject of Gregory's bank book was the furthest thing from her mind. In fact the two things may well have been connected.

∞

Padgett looked at his own skin. It did not look right, did not look hard and fast, secure, watertight, soultight, Weggstight. Could it roll off the bones in curds and separates of released being? As well as trundling away into the slow setting, the setting also created itself, brought itself gradually into existence. A pioneer and his wagon vanishing from slow sight towards a no man's land in hope of fool's gold or great cattle ranches ... the setting of a soul into a horizon only he knew existed.

He'd dossed there, dossed here, dossed all over the place, in all times and conditions of his own choosing, like a god of a god that was him. No achievements except that of achieving failure as an acceptance speech to himself. And the corrupting skin continued to roll back to reveal the Weirdmonger and, in scatologies of vexed text, he screamed: 'Bring it on!' And the trundling continued overland where indigenes were speaking in weirdtongues only understandable if one could listen enough to one's own in-built Tor of Babel as it overviewed the wide riparian realities of fiction and astrogony as they (these realities) threaded the white-water nemonities in chase of some great eschatological hare of meaning or noumenon between banks of whimsy and nonsense. Banks built from half-rotted bookspines.

∞

Despite interferences, Gregory's life rather entered a plateau stage where mundane matters continued to prevail. He sorted out his mother. He loved her dearly but wept buckets at how thoughtless she was. She was ever the sucker for the con man with a fast buck business scheme needing investment. But this last one was the last straw. A fat man who wanted to set up a series of fattening food outlets all over recently tariff-free Middle Europe took the ticket. He wasn't even good looking and hid all his defects under a jolly confidence in the ways of business … and of love. He had absconded with all Gregory's savings which Gregory had entrusted to the 'power of attorney' of his mother whilst he was *non compos mentis* in hospital. Why had he entrusted them to his mother of all people? He had nobody else. And, despite all the examples of why he shouldn't trust her, he did trust her. Mothers were like that. She had brought him up on a pittance and, despite exposing him to all manner of drunken step-fathers and the intermittent periods of her ignoring Gregory completely, she had seen them both through. Gregory was Gregory because he was his mother's son. She deserved trust even if she couldn't be trusted.

Suzie couldn't be trusted. He often doubted she existed at all. Just wishful thinking that he could hold down a relationship. Yet she was there most of the time. Proof was in the eyes, both their eyes. He should have given his bank book to her, no doubt. But she didn't have his blood, his provenance. She and her own mother were pawns in a bigger game they didn't understand. A game which even Gregory himself, at the moment, didn't understand.

Gregory shrugged. He almost preferred it when he wasn't being sensible. Sensible meant worrying, having concerns, form-filling, lying awake at night with no possibility of dreams, linear plots of life, practicalities, no imagination, no risk taking, no vision sharing, no circuses, no clowns…

∞

The clown with a black rosette in his flirty lapel was removing the masking cream from his face. Tomorrow they would be lowering the rigging of the Big Top ready for trundling away from this caravanserai to another. He was deeply honourable, deeply serious, yet acting the fool made him feel that he was ever plotting against the unplottable or representing a 'clandestiny' that made him a spy amid the frighteningly absurd existentialism around him—and, in the end, it was not laughs he was after, but sobs. Maybe not even sobs, but cries of terror and despair. And that need in him to hurt, of course, hurt him more than if he wasn't honourable, wasn't serious.

Nevertheless, he took no blame for the pretty trapezist's fall, because he had earlier retightened the loose pinion in the airy gods of the tall wide tent. He had done this primarily, however, because he knew there was no point in booby-trapping himself. You see, soon after the original business with disabling the props, he was told by the Weirdmonger to act as replacement ringmaster (instead of being clown) for that evening's performance …

There was nothing worse for a clown to be. Tears were in his eyes like wobbly transparent snailshells. Let's hope (he hoped) that, in the new catchment area for the Circus, real ringmasters would not be too thin on the ground.

∞

Feemy formed newer and newer fats the more he was described, as if the words themselves—employed by many writers to characterise his body and mind—were ingested by the noumenal construction of 'Feeminess', swelling it beyond its otherwise normal configuration as a real or normal person. In other words, Blasphemy 'Feemy' Fitzworth—the legendary cat's meat man who was once so lean and fit—became the very vein-proud mound of pulsing meat itself that he once used to sell (when diced into chosen cuts) as a supply of the cheap piecemeals for any Victorian pets parented within the precincts of Dickensian London.

Rachel 'Chelly' Mildeyes—one of the many tiny child-followers of Feemy's ancient costermongering—was, of course, the keenest hero-worshipping example of those 'pied-pipered' urchins who not only enjoyed being darkened by Feemy's shadow but also slipshod by his meatcart's greasy trail. However, now, today, in her older and wordier time of life, Chelly has eventually become one of the many writers who threw (and still throws) merging masses of meaning in his direction, not only serving to bloat out his shape, but changing that shape's very personality from an erstwhile energetic time-traveller—one who heroically hunted down monsters that other writers had gratuitously thrown to the 'reality' wind to subsist as new plagues—into one of those very monsters he once thus hunted!

∞

Gregory spent many days trying to spin untruths about the past (or unspin truths). This helped him reconcile some of his own behaviour—behaviour which was ostensibly so out-of-character—with his own views of his mother's attempts to make castles from the shifting sands of her fading love-life. For Gregory, on the other hand, Suzie (his own love-life) was a time-line to a trapeze-act which he could actually hope to grasp in the future. They together followed the Weirdmonger's circus and its head-clown—a clown who, when in non-clown civvies, sported a black rosette and a cross-ply three-piece suit (whatever the weather)—to other towns and other sites in even stranger parks. Gregory told Suzie he wanted to be a ringmaster, after all. Suzie—in some bemused response more fitting for a 'Big Brother' contestant—said he would do well in the Circus of the Tourettes (as it was called) and she would tease out support for him when approaching the caravan or medicine-wagon where such decisions were made. Diary-rooms were not always purpose-built, you see. *Dairy*-rooms, too, as the bovine racers slowed to a near-halt towards the border between reality and fiction.

∞

Padgett Weggs shed yet another carapace of self as he wandered London's haunts. The whole of history became a circus—a flighty kaleidoscope on one hand, a droning bomb-alley on the other hand. Middle-Fast fighters churning across the sky in the hope of finding the saint who carried his own skin.

∞

Rachel squinted, making her eyeballs feel like snails trying to escape gooey shells. She was at least as old as these bowls of sight: now milky-grey on the surface but with glimpses of ancient feistiness that gave little suspicion of the deceptive mildness of her youthful glances.

She was essentially her own language that she had grown to name Weirdtongue. However, having been given the language or, rather, captured by the language, it actually named itself from her own lips or writing-nibs. Many years a student of the bibliographic catalogues that she so meticulously itemised in her own special carrel at the University of Tourettes Library, she eventually found herself steeped in the various byways and mazes of the wordprint's lettering itself: a vexed texture of text that had trapped her in its trammels even though she once started life as a simple-minded soul clad by Chellyhood, one who traipsed after city costermongers amid other trilling and cooing urchins of the streets: trying to wring sustenance from the dried-out poverties of fate.

Working out how she had ended up in a University Library as a cataloguer made the sense of each shorter sentence trip out more clearly. The words unravelled into linear stretches of healthy and unmistakeable meaning. She had a knack at the art of logical pigeon-holing and, during the Flew Plagues, she suddenly slipped through a meathole left by the careless Feemy Fitzworth straight into the timeless pursuits of clerical / administrative work and general office duties in a more mundane world at the edge of Victorian London not too far into its future, indeed a tiny tangent of time in the form of one of those transparent sticky corners for pasting snapshots into a photo album.

Rachel eventually married Charles Fitzworth—Feemy's brother—and gave birth to Suzie. Rachel herself had been ill lately with added complications of thought. As had Suzie's boy friend, Gregory. Now Rachel was worried that Gregory (having been prematurely released from hospital) was leading her astray by following fortunes that even Dick Whittington would have refused to follow, cat or no cat. Yet, it all made perfect sense, with most complications now gone. And she smiled—not at her worries about her daughter Suzie that she tried to put out of her mind—but at the clarity of her own thoughts, untouched (hopefully) by any taint of vexed texture of text. She did not need to put out of her mind that Gregory's own mother was caught up in the business ventures of an ever-fattening Feemy Fitzworth because, despite Rachel's seeming omniscience, she had no idea about these unlikely coincidental connections between the protagonists of her now renewed encroachment of vexed texture of text as she desperately spiralled her fountain pen towards the end of the latest page, with all hope of straightforward sentences of thought now flown completely out the library window into the night.

Rachel slept, head cornered by her arms resting on the carrel table. She needed to sleep off any further vexing of her audit trails. Simplicity became the only cure for an imaginary sickness that was often mistaken for dreaming. Later, upon waking into this renewal of simplicity, she explored the books themselves, rather than merely listing them into a catalogue. This act of listing, in the normal course of events, was the only remedy for complications, but now that she had indeed regathered her own natural simplicity she could actually *read* the books with impunity, rather than just listing them. She was unable to find any record of informal Dream Sickness or its complications technically named Nemophilia or Nemophobia. It was as if these illnesses had never existed. Medical books were only for hypochondriacs, in any event. She sighed with relief as simplicity continued to flood back into her soul, fading her complications until, eventually, they were written in invisible ink. Any antipodal angst, meanwhile, became funnels of real visible ink pouring away anti-clockwise through the newly released vent of her over-active imagination.

∞

Gregory and Suzie arrived on foot—as the Tor and its hill slowly disappeared behind a duskful of mist, a phenomenon that reminded them of full-blown night sown with melted light crystals from earlier dreams. The circus tent, recently pitched in a nearby field, was almost as big as the Tor and its hill put together, with the canvas filled by a lambency that betokened the dress rehearsals of the acts within. The myriad of caravan windows created glints or sparkles in contrast to the huge uniformity of the canvas canyon glowing by their side.

'I wonder which one?' said Gregory. He looked at Suzie, both of them tired and smeared by their mixture of walking and hitch-hiking since leaving London. Sleeping rough like many such rough sleepers who were already in the vicinity of the tent in readiness for the whole festival of which the circus was the focus. Not only rough sleepers on the spur of the moment's excitement, but also professional dossers who felt at home in such a gathering.

'Which one?' echoed Suzie. 'Which caravan? I expect it's the one nearest the tent.'

Gregory suddenly felt a surge of depression as he realised there would be much more competition for the role of ringmaster than he anticipated when it had first been mooted that there was a ringmaster shortage—but, of course, that had been in the snootier parts of London. Here, however, it would not be a foregone conclusion, after all. During such preambles of misfired decision-making, Gregory suddenly stumbled over one of the rough sleepers or dossers, little hoping that this was the man he had really come to meet. Suzie had meanwhile taken up with a non-sleeping group nearer the tent, evidently some trapeze-artists trying to persuade her to train with them, as she must have looked lithely attractive and potentially air-borne. Their light prattle of gossip moved the light crystals about with the renewed glint of fireflies or fairies but, then, Suzie glanced back to see if Gregory was making any progress towards his own aims of a circus life, but saw only a pair of snaky shadows slithering into one. Or was that Gregory there being led by the hand in the company of a sharp-suited gentleman sporting a black rosette in his lapel? Nobody could tell the chiefs from the indians in this ever-darkening arena beneath the Tor, especially as each disguised the other by the careless merging of identities as once happened when London was first evacuated by the use of false or interchangeable labels on suitcases and satchels.

∞

It is difficult to pinpoint the precise moment when Feemy Fitzworth no longer needed a physical meatcart to tote his wares around Victorian London—but, if pinpointed, it was the moment when he became the meatcart himself. So many words had been ingested by his 'persona', swelling his glands into even fattier tissues—and he used the steaming heat of the weather that often attacked London in those days to cook the slices he would later slice from his belly quarters and hocks from his hind-calves and heifers from his humpback. A walking carvery.

But without the words he would never have found himself in such a (lucky?) position where he was a self-perpetuating purveyor of cat's meat for the clipped-back folk of Lower Thames Street. The words used on his behalf immediately turned into fat or flesh or sometimes pre-cooked meat upon his previously lean-shanked hams as soon as they hit the vicinity of his mean gait in front of the soon-to-be-discarded meatcart, discarded, at first, by becoming a *ghostly* meatcart being towed behind him amid the excited imaginary coos and shrieks of now ghostly children, who had died from food poisoning or simply been stuck up chimney-flues. The cart later—in dreams if not in ghostly form—soon took on the traits of the Weirdmonger's medicine wagon on Weirdmonger Wheels. Cat's meat liquidised into doses of linctus to stave off Flew or Quinsy. But then, when the shape of a giant circus tent grew from the canvas wagon, Feemy left the dream before it finished, and dreamed of other things, like the tall Captain Bintiff and his way of talking Weirdtongue. Then, as already indicated, Feemy became the meatcart himself simply because the words said so.

Yet, worse dreams returned to frique and vex the mind of Feemy. He could not endure the strain of toting himself round the streets as a mound of steaming dung disguised as meat (as it later became). He would often doze off within the shade of St Paul's Dome during the unseemly summers that a backward echo of global warming surprisingly caused without any history books noticing … listening to the ghostly Luftwaffe bombers from the future, while pre-filling the role that Padgett Weggs would later play in a similar position on the pavement (60 years' hence) as he filled out the silhouette that had once been Feemy's.

Captain Bintiff stood statuesque against his own larger silhouette, wagging a huge protuberance from his mouth—a rude gesture that Feemy wondered if the school playground chant would be spell enough to ward off the curses from the

sound of language thus produced: *Sticks and stones may break my bones, but names or words will never change me.*
Or even ringtones.

∞

Gregory Mummerset woke at dawn. He and Suzie Mildeyes had pitched their tiny tent when it was really too dark to do so—and the rain that had seeped in towards their sleeping-bags they blamed on their own amateurish efforts of tightening the guy-ropes rather than on the low quality of the tent itself. They always bought things too cheaply. The *buy one get one free* mentality that meant people these days put up with shoddy goods just for the sake of a bargain. They feared the ground would become muddy which was an unwelcome feature of the festival held here for some years now in the shadow of the Tor.

Upon yawning, he crawled from the front flap, pleasantly surprised that the sunlight had replaced the rain with its own promising shadows that had nothing to do with the shadows of the night before. Earlier darknesses had been shaken off with the change in direction of his thoughts. Suzie slithered in his wake, then stretching as she stood, smiling at the new atmosphere and the fresh concerns. Many other campers travelled on their bellies to leave their overnight shelters ... some with guitars strapped to their backs.

The larger tent that held one of the performing stages was glistening with dew. In the distance, they squinted to see the larger erection of scaffolding which would later bear the main acts. 'Goldwrap' was headlining tonight, the group they had come all this way to see. See and hear. Seeing music was the only way to hear it, especially if there was more to the music than just the sound. Gregory enjoyed loud music when it was in enclosed spaces veritably vibrating the ribs of his body. It was only then he could actually feel he was living *within* the music. He rather doubted that open fields or tents would do justice to the claustrophobia he felt was needed to contain the sounds.

Goldwrap's supporting group 'Nemophilia' that was already rehearsing in the nearby tent (currently closed to the public) filled the fields with haphazard shafts of jagged music startled from synths. Either tuning up or the real thing, Gregory wasn't sure. In his quieter moments, he rather enjoyed Classical Music, even the more avant garde versions to which one needed to acclimatise (almost self-brainwash) before the seemingly strident sounds reached the parts of the soul most other music couldn't reach. He also enjoyed the sedate conversations of chamber music ... Schubert, Brahms. Then, in other moods, the decadent prefiguring of modern warfare in turn-of-the-century Mahler followed by moto perpetuos by Shostakovich. 'Death In Venice' music by Mahler reminded him of his earlier dreams-of-promise visiting all the Middle European health spas as part of a necessary convalescence from too much dreaming. The mountains were pulmonaries of shiver-veined delight.

He shook off his own shivers—on this fresh morning after a close-stitched night of dripping canvas—by taking Suzie in his arms. He kissed her lightly on the lips and then looked into her eyes that were aglow, awet even, with both a waking love and a desire to live life for every moment it could give them free from any cloying dream. They were, for once, real. They were here. And, as Nemophobia took sway with true rhythms of pre-cast musical score rather than improvisation, they drew breath to lengthen their next kiss together.

Gregory and Suzie, hand in hand, left the communal tented area to visit the various side-shows and sales-stalls and other New Age paraphernalia, whilst listening to a mix of rehearsals blending in and out of each other as the distances changed the angle of each musical attack. Some music—great music—is fiction injected straight into the vein, thought Gregory.

The fields came to life with birdsong—not to be outdone by the music—and other animal life urged forward to graze both in the stylised shapes of the configured landscape and for real as living breathing creatures. Lowing cows traipsed in a line up the slopes towards the Tor itself, a slow race, a becoming breed.

∞

'Wagger Market! Wagger Market! Come to Wagger Market!'

The salescries—distant cousins of the strident costermongery in the streets of earlier England—echoed from stall to stall in the light of the shortening shadows. An ice-cream van also interspersed such cries with its own tacky ring-a-ding-ding tunes as it wended from one side of the site to the other hoping that the heat of the morning would fill mouths with more than just mutual desire.

The Weirdmonger had set up his own stall selling the traditional rudery in proud-veined shanks hung upon the vertical canvas-counter shivering in the hot wind and allowing individual items of fleshy dislocations of such rudery to shake and rattle like a Cuban backing-track: a sound seemingly at ease with the random rehearsals of emergent music from various stages being set up around the outskirts of the market.

The Weirdmonger's stall rarely sold rudery 'on the hoof'—but, today, he was pleased with some of his 'living' stock—as opposed to the usual oven-ready or 'new body'-ready amputations and castrations. This being a major selling opportunity during the Glistenberry Festival, many of his wares, this morning, were, therefore, still attached to the people whence they would soon be freshly ripped given a successful sale. Many figures stood with their tongues hanging out in the hope of paying customers for these fleshy pink flannels they had been known to fatten up with bits of real human lung or animal lights or simply words.

Captain Bintiff was the main mannequin—just for show like those huge flagons of coloured liquid that used to appear in ancient Chemist-shop windows—standing tallishly beside the Weirdmonger with his mouth appendage teasingly tipping out and withdrawn then flashing out like a snake in full length, fleetingly glimpsed then withdrawn again—thus tempting buyers to the stall with this intermittent rudery. Blowing kisses and then snarling. Raising his Captain's hat, bowing then spitting viciously. All showmanship. Crude tongue-sticking at its artistic best.

Gregory and Suzie eschewed approaching the stall with the rudery. Perhaps they suspected echoes of something they wanted to forget. Or perhaps it was because the Weirdmonger had no special *buy one get one free* offers.

∞

Still within his night's billet of self-ballooned air near Wagger Market, Padgett Weggs tossed and turned, dossed and dreamed, tossed and turned again, over-dosing, indeed, on dreaming of Feemy Fitzworth dreaming of Padgett dreaming of Feemy both of whom were dreamed in turn by other snatch-within-snatches of dreamers till one reached, by inference, the head-lease dreamer.

'A human body, like my own body,' Padgett dreamed a voice saying in his own voice, 'is something you can't get off. A bodytrap. I'm inside it and there is nothing I can do to escape it. Then the bodytrap further swells with the words used to describe it yet inexplicably tighter and tighter around my shrinking self. To escape its trammels would be certain death. I wonder how I ended up like this in such a nightmare. Knowing it's all going to end with a 'blank'—while incapable of waking up from the dream that this is so.

I remember many dreams I thought were real at the time I was dreaming them like this one I'm describing for you, nightmares with terrifying situations I thought I could never escape—until, with great relief, I would indeed wake up and leave it all behind as a quickly forgotten dream. Life's real problems are as nothing compared to those real-seeming problems one sometimes meets in dreams. But this waking nightmare of the bodytrap, all our bodytraps, is not a dream you can wake up from. It's relentlessly and terrifyingly inescapable. Who the devil landed me in this body with their words? They have a lot to answer for. And I can't really imagine the devastating effect of complete and utter non-existence when this consciousness that is me within my body finally vanishes as it surely will. A paradox—that we hate being trapped in our bodies and find it a devastating imposition to be thus trapped—but we'd give anything to stay trapped there forever, because we can't face the outright 'blankness' if we cease being trapped there!'

An answering voice: 'Our faces are pressed up against the mortal shell like a child wanting to go out to play but kept indoors like the 'invalid' in *The Secret Garden*.'

A third voice: 'Life is indeed an imposition but you need life itself to realise the imposition has been tricked on you when you weren't looking!'

A fourth voice (a real one waking the dreamers): 'Wagger Market! Wagger Market! Come To Wagger Market!'

Followed by the shivering of ringtones.

∞

One stall was headed up 'Ringmaster'—behind the counter of which stood a man in a sharp suit sporting a black wind-teased rosette in a loose-flapped lapel. The rosette was particularly improminent bearing in mind the colour of the suit. Gregory failed to notice it, whilst Suzie noticed it but without noting it. Their eyes were more for what the rosette-bearer sold. Make-up still stained the bags under his eyes, despite an attempt at earlier removal with unmasking-cream but Gregory and Suzie were not to notice that till later.

The stall's wares were rings of all sorts. Rings as light- or heavy-weight cosmetics for fingers. Some flange or rivet rings. All in different metals with or without precious stones embedded. There were food rings, like doughnuts. Avant garde or artistic rings like rancid meat in continuous sausages and rings of what looked like human flesh but rather more respectable than the rudery they had just been inspecting on a previous stall and rings that were balloons filled with air worthy of any circus act or juggling with smoke-rings or sculpting into elastic shapes of interlocking rings by prestidigitation or sleight-of-hand. A ring cycle—where the motive force was derived from stepping along with the whole body inside the rim of the ring. And other more unrecognisable rings bordering on the edge of not being rings at all.

They bought a ring cycle each with a view to easing their passage around the festival site. The rain did not look as if it were returning, so mud would not be a problem, they thought. The stall-holder did warn them that these devices were not good in mud … unless one further invested in 'snow-tracking' spindles to act as a gritting device outside the rim of the ring. Gregory and Suzie—after a little tiff—decided on eschewal of the tracking and then slowly and precariously step-wheeled off amid their own giggles and suffering stares from other festival-goers.

'Good God!' said Gregory. 'There's the lead-singer of Goldwrap!'

Suzie looked to see someone fleet past in their own ring-cycle, evidently far more proficient at such self-transport than Suzie and Gregory.

'How do you know it was her?'

'She called out 'ooh-la-la, I'm the number one'!' He laughed as if he hadn't really convinced himself as to the true identity of the other ring-cyclist. Followed by a non-sequitur that he'd rather like to have Goldwrap music as a mobile ringtone.

∞

Death is a hobby. I try to collect death stamps as well as death rings. I have an old-fashioned mobile with a tiny ring-dial into which I can't put my fingers for navigating its numbered holes and I await the final call from our maker for the due date of my death rather than me ringing Him first. Instead, much later, after years of waiting for the call, a letter came with a death stamp in its top right-hand corner bearing a symbol that would later turn out to be very important. A symbol that would remain a mystery till this book has illustrations or artwork because, so far, words have never really been enough to firm up the intangibilities as easily as they had fattened Feemy.

Modal Morales looked into a mirror ringed with the lit colours of electric bayonet bulbs. He removed the rosette, as his thoughts drifted back from the screensaver of dreams that he usually could ignore due to the numbness of its familiarity—yet retaining, without volition, the echo of the symbol that had not been dreamed properly—a strange phenomenon, as one would have thought it easier to remember things that *had* been dreamed properly.

He started painting his face, affixing the bulbous red nose, and black rouge on the cheeks, and popping shut a line of black rosettes down the front of his baggy 'Andy Pandy' suit. He would be on stage with that night's headlining group in just one hour. Nerves were not often Modal's bag. But tonight he was unexpectedly anxious. He looked at his passport as if to gain confidence from his own identity, proud of some of the visas branded on the watermarked pages.

Death has more to offer when a mirror reflects the face that would soon be dead: not a synergy as such but a love affair with incidence. Fatted calves crawling further up the legs to corrupt the genitals.

∞

In a piece of music by Charles Ives, the sounds of a small-town celebration are represented—i.e. competing marching bands, political discussions, fireworks and women unloading picnic baskets. Yet this was as nothing compared to what the tall silhouetted figure of Abraham Bintiff heard as he stood Tor-like on the hill above dawn-glit Glistenberry. Yet even if he heard fireworks, none could be seen. Rehearsals on various stages set up around the site did however contribute to the impression of competing bands.

Earlier in the twilight of dusk and (again) dawn itself both of which seemed to have one flash of pure darkness between, those milling about the festival site would have glimpsed up and saw Bintiff whom they took to be the familiar dark tower spasmodically poking a huge whip of deeper darkness into a lashing of the stars. Without realising it, as they fell into hushes of puzzled awe, they spoke their own versions of the Weirdtongue and Goldwrap languages, mixed with the shifting frames of music as the often strident rhapsodies and pavanes moved in and out of each other with equally purposeful and random reflections of what was later to happen in our growing story of Bintiff's ensuing battle with the clown Modal Morales. That plot of a battle itself would have its own battle with another plot, i.e. the adventures of Feemy Fitzworth as he wandered, like a centaur, the more oblique corners of our vexed texture of text, trying to sell his own steaming hindquarters as cat's meat.

∞

'Don't you just love new words that take root...?' stuttered Chelly Mildeyes accompanied by her blonde-haired amanuensis, as they both sat down at the table. Chelly's back hurt and it showed. It was cramped in the makeshift carrel behind the Glistenberry Festival's main performance area. Despite her great age, she did not intend to dominate the proceedings. Yet they did need a chairperson to steer matters quickly before the next group took to the stage and released the relentless rhythms of their circus-themed glamrock act. Then nobody would be able to hear themselves speak.

The participants of the conference had arrived at the site inspecting their ill-fastened late-labels tied on their satchels or briefcases, as they had been rushed here from various centres of creativity before tidying up their own lives, let alone anybody else's life in the real or fictitious worlds of which they had been given at least temporary charge. They were all ostensibly writers but one or two of them could not remember writing anything.

In delayed response to Chelly's opening gambit, Padgett Weggs fidgeted awkwardly in his stained sleeping-bag as he tried to make it (with him in it) fit into a chair. He was cold despite the heat. He was always cold. Something to do with what he thought had been written about him, and what he would write about himself given the chance. Then said: 'Yes, rockgroups here need some new names to get them noticed.' He laughed. 'What about Weirdmonger...' He glanced to another conference participant who bore that very label. 'Megazanthus? Weirdtongue? The Tenacity Of Feathers? Klaxon City? The Hawler? The Mutts? Lovecraft?...'

'There was once a group called HP Lovecraft,' proffered an inscrutable old man with a moonface, beard, glasses, mole on left cheek. '...but should we not get down to the main item on the agenda?'

'That being the battle of plots?' excoriated the Weirdmonger with a sneer, grabbing back the words he'd just uttered (with the delayed addition of a question mark) before they became irretrievable truths. He did not want them wasted on the current company. Even single neologisms from his mouth became separate believable dictionaries of semantic force. He gnawed on one of his own wares from his stall, an item of amputated rudery turned into a sausage ring capable of edibility with or without its continuous core of rancid gristle which (if present) could be eschewed before corrupting the palate.

'Well, we want to sell this serial to the TV companies—and we need to agree on where it's going...' said another old man with a much longer beard and narrower face. 'And we need to be clearer not only about its direction but the language used. Vexed texture of text? Weirdtongue? Phooey! Clarity is everything.'

There were many cups of tea and cakes handed out around the table. But this did not indicate it was a tea party.

'I suggest we concentrate on Feemy Fitzworth as a centaur or living meatcart,' suddenly said Padgett Weggs, 'because ... well ... I think he is part of myself and I can tell you things about him that even he himself wouldn't know. Undreamabilities of depth. We could have him wandering the fantastical lands of the world selling cat's meat and meeting adventures. An illimitable amount of it the more words we use. The more the merrier. Get those words working!'

'I think there is more mileage in a brand new character—that clown ... what is he called? Modal Morales? And the rejuvenescence of an older character—Captain Bintiff—now with a long tongue. There is much potential dramatic tension there and an impending battle between them that could be quite spectacular as an ending. A far sparer, clearer...' (a nod towards the gent who had spoken about clarity) '...outcome and path towards that outcome...' The last speaker, Jane Turpin, in satin chic—sitting next to Chelly Mildeyes as her amanuensis and spokesperson—sighed as these and other comments were overtaken by loud strumming from the nearby stage together with a startlement of synths. The conference participants stared into their teas as the makeshift carrel began to shake. One of them, however, started to tear his notes and ran off...

Gregory and Suzie (divorced from any proceedings of debate or questionable direction) stood at the back of the equally makeshift audience as the next group's lead singer strutted towards the mike. A few large bovine animals with human heads followed in dance routine as the synths recovered from their own startled beginnings—and a clown with black rosettes down his baggy front and with mispainted cheeks took uncertain charge of a mock keyboard as a ludicrous prop while the lead singer herself entered a fine series of preparatory trills. The participants of the audience held up luminous items of marine snail-life and waved them in the air like peace candles amid the darkness which would nevertheless fail to shift ... moving in time to the resonant driving chords that shook their own human ribs in increasing volume. The tenuous sky somehow (by a magic fiction slowly emerging from its shell of magic realism) acted as a cathedral-roof or cut-off point echoing back the sounds satisfyingly, if deafeningly. This was a group called Gilded Fripperies, Gregory discovered from a torn snail-lit programme planted in his hand by someone who had suddenly appeared out of nowhere. Yet the distant drumkit said 'Gelded' not 'Gilded' ... or 'Geldof'. Too far to see properly.

∞

Following attendance at the festival's main stage, Gregory Mummerset and Suzie Mildeyes later yearned for the more gentle melody of lullabies rather than the thumping thumbprints of sound pressed into the soft-imagined carapaces of their once new-born heads. They returned to their tent along with raging migraines: potential op-art dreameries if sleep should help to dull the pains alongside its more customary provision of creative gliding through the fripperies of unreality.

They had enjoyed the 'circus' stage-show but the delayed diminishment of competing sounds—rehearsed as well as unrehearsed—from all corners of the benighted site did little to encourage the curative qualities of sleep. The tent was cross-skewed itself as if hordes had skirted it during the collateral damage caused by some ill-reported war here among the valleys and beneath the long-tongued Tor. The ground's mildewy discomfort gave sleep further excuse to keep poking from its shell, antennae quivering in search of further delay.

The couple looked pitifully into each other's eyes; leaning forward from time to time while lightly kissing away the tears. They were out of depth. Gregory even feared he might need to return to the hospital. Mildeyes and melody-boxes. Somersaults and summersets. The cavortings of a clown. A group called Friques in a side-tent. Safety-net spiders spinning big tops for pops. Marionettes hanging half-dead between the tangling spools of sleep's slow withdrawal and the crazy-paved merging of two migraines. The incredible Mister Kite. A dark shadow swooping in…

∞

Blasphemy Fitzworth was aboard the fair-sailed *Glittenburier* as it entered a new harbour of choice without visible steam or sound. Captain Bintiff had long since left this particular texture of truth upon the original craft of Feemy's destiny with a crew chosen from several of the other voyages that had since intervened yet remained strangely unreported by any of our correspondents in the field. Where Bintiff had gone, nobody in these parts even pretended to know. Feemy's new Captain if he had a long tongue certainly hid it with a short one. As hidden as his name. A nemophile with emptiness for a face.

Despite the beauty of the fantastical turrets (each a hilltopping Tor in its own right) built upon each new brow of dream, there was a wholesale war afoot here, too, and here and here—with many wild machinations of politick and bent magick. Feemy tried to retain his innocent task of selling meaty parts of himself to the natives—but natives who prided themselves as more civilised than Feemy felt they had no need of such meagre off-cuttings of grease and gristle. They had edible luxuries (rich in protein) hidden within their own humps, but failed to be able to reach round to mine them. Yet, simply knowing luxuries were there (just behind them) made the natives feel confident enough to near starve rather than buy provender from the likes of Feemy.

These natives were native of nowhere. Nemophobes in the main, however, they vigorously sought a name for the land that Feemy had now reached as well as names for themselves ... names for the land where they (these as yet nameless ones) purportedly lived amid the mass of hilltopping Tors and nightly-lit circuses and festivals galore in each valley cleft. If any reader has a name for this land and its natives before we visit its veils and piques again, please let it be known. If, indeed, any reader wishes actually to enter as a real character into the throes of the story towards bolstering, even curing, these various vexed textures of destiny or truth known as Weirdtongue, please also make yourself known to the narrative hospital.

∞

They said Gregory had an interesting name. Mummerset was unusual yet real, unlike Suzie's 'Mildeyes' concocted from nice-sounding words like Mild and Eyes and Melodies and not so nice like Mildewy, as inherited from her mother Rachel (Chelly), whilst Suzie's biological father Churles Fitzworth was not even acknowledged as a person let alone a name. Feemy indeed never had a brother at all let alone one called Churles except possibly the tumorous hump he called a backpack. Facts that make fiction tick. Nemophilia laced with its opposite.

When in the Narrative Hospital, Gregory, as you will recall, had been promised subsequent recuperation in Middle Europe with trial convalescences in each of its famous health spas, including the Magic Mountain in Austria, the Yellow Valley in Poland, the White Water Retreat in Slovenia, the Middle-Eye Clinic in Slovakia and even as far west as the Swiss Alps where more nameless institutions paraded as Concentration Camps that never really existed except, perhaps, in the rough-cuts of Padgett Weggs' imagination.

Whilst recovering from the night's concert in the tented village, Gregory remembered the promise made to him so glibly at the hospital. He wondered if promises once made fade away to nothing compared to the real promises they once were when first spoken. Promises should be in writing.

'The promise must be in writing somewhere,' said Suzie. 'I'm sure I read about the spas somewhere. On paper headed with the hospital's name and signed by someone in charge …'

'Well, one would have thought so, wouldn't you? Because things that are simply promised into the heat of the air are little better than fairy tales!' Gregory looked stern. They had enjoyed the show by Modal Morales and his group but now, like promises themselves, any sights and sounds were quickly fading, the stage names not only fading but changing as time passed. He remembered being visited at the hospital by the Weirdmonger who wrote a few things out on the carrel table for Gregory, not only descriptions, but prescriptions, too. But a hospital visitor is necessarily several rungs below 'someone-in-charge', even though this particular visitor did have his own medicine wagon. Maybe the signed papers had been left behind in Gregory's flat—or given to one of their mothers for safe-keeping. They both laughed at the unspoken thought.

They took a breather outside the tent—as more oxygen could ease headaches. The Tor stood sentinel on its hill, now tongueless as proper dreams resumed and the made-up ones faded.

∞

Darkness and humour feed off each other. I often feel I'm darker the funnier I've been. The universe itself is a porridge-pot full of jokes and dreams—smudged or smeared with blood like jam upon its lumpy surface. An empty pot would leave me only with despair itself, a despair no more productive of darkness than anything else. Filling the pot— i.e. with a porridge of jokes and other bric-a-brac of life— brings out the concept of true despair, a deeper despair because you can't reach deep enough into the pot to grab it and thus test out how truly it's despair itself. An easily discovered despair which exists in the form of an obvious despair amid its own emptiness can be measured and contained and eventually dissipated. I shall have no truck with despair so easily measured or dissipated. I want my despair hidden or filled by jokes and dreameries of life—and thus it becomes a deeper, direr and more dreadful despair ... forever.

Not even death can reach the despair. Or stop the jokes.

∞

Feemy Fitzworth reached another corner in his life, sailing into the predominantly land-locked countries of Middle Europe. River courses were sometimes hardly wide enough for the *'Glittenburier'* to negotiate but the Captain was astute enough to treat them like the open sea: a cumulation of rivers, a culmination of currents as a single current. Thus, the ship reached territories normally closed to ships, opening new markets for self-perpetuated meat that allowed Feemy to text back to Mrs Mummerset in England that he was making their combined fortunes. Her investment was safe.

But then the ship reached the Yellow Valley purported to be in Poland but, in actual fact, strung along its exact borders with elsewhere. In these parts, many convalescents and invalids and consumptives were banned the use of meat and forced to eat nothing but rocket salad. They were also told to breathe the pulmonaries day and night to send the mountain air in sick wafts towards an ancient city where a trumpeter marked the time of day by emerging sporadically from the top of a church tower like a cuckoo from a Swiss clock. Feemy was captured and press-ganged into hidden kitchen duties for clandestine midnight feasts that the inmates of the Yellow Valley health spa arranged so as to staunch their craving for meat. Meanwhile, the *'Glittenburier'* sailed on Feemilessly towards Modern Samarkand.

∞

The Glistenberry site was eventually empty, its tussocks hustled by a dry wind—but a few residual ring-cyclists crisscrossed the dark arena where once the biggest tent was pitched. But it turned out they were ghosts of ring-cyclists and some of them even stayed ring-cycling during the twilit preamble to sunrise—their feet pitifully pedalling like hamsters in water-wheels—seeking not only their real selves but also the joys they once possessed when the festival was in full swing. Even the mud was dried into cracked sculptures of itself and made to lie silent below an imaginary blanket of rock music echoing from the past in potential conflict with the more gentle threnodies of nature's renewal. Some cyclists even fell out of their rings in an ungainly fashion but, mercifully, because the main advantage of existing as a ghost was being largely immune to embarrassment, they just as quickly vanished into thin air where any form of embarrassment was not relevant given the fact they might have remained to suffer embarrassment had it not been for that quickly forgotten moment of overlapping embarrassment and non-embarrassment at the precise point of vanishment that ghosts could only manage by blushing first.

Other than the ghosts, two figures of male persuasion—accompanied by a blonde-haired young lady whom we once knew as Jane—were now seen to cross the derelict site in officious stride. One was inordinately tall and silent. Not tongue-tied as such, but consciously stern and serious, as if words would fill him with unwanted meaning. The other was shorter and had swollen cheeks, sporting a black rosette in the lapel of his sharp suit. He appeared to be talking to himself to allow his cheeks to subside but the silence nevertheless prevailed. Jane carried a basket with two guns lying side by side like lovers. The men would need two seconds before the rituals of battle could ensue and she was now talking frantically on her mobile in an attempt to create more time or to kill time, both of which really meant the same thing.

∞

Many miles from Glistenberry, the Yellow Valley wound like a dried-out ribbon of land between once high man-made riverbanks, vaguely considered to be a continuous groove or growth of pre-civilisation interfering with some of the more vicious geographies of racial history in the middle contours of the twentieth-century. Many local rumours, however, were better accredited, inasmuch as they claimed that the common weather conditions thereabouts gave the valley configuration's name its colour and had no bearing on the outcome of any wars in or out of history books. But some competing formal histories (rather more political than geographical) suggested, rather less certainly than the rumours, that there was a single man (a national hero to some, the direst villain to others) bearing a name that was a vague colour followed by a misty vision self-defeatedly veiling the very histories that seemed to prove he once existed. A name currently so vague, it is impossible yet to interfere with its delayed crystallisation till it (the name) appears in person during any attempts at recording how the world changed as a result of his deeds and any bearing these deeds had on Feemy's sojourn in Middle Europe.

Feemy, meanwhile, was still serving secret feasts at the Yellow Valley health clinic—using his own meat by a regular bloody tweezering of his difficult-to-reach hocks and hams ... yet not telling anyone whence the meat came for fear of being accused of force-feeding cannibals. Soon, however, the words that could be spared for describing Feemy and his doings would very likely soon run out—thus diminishing any further fattening of his person and the consequent meat on or off the bone. And without meat, he would be without a job. Words would be needed elsewhere in view of the fact that the sheaf of official papers—which Feemy surreptitiously read when they were accidentally left in one of the clinic's carrels—stated that a patient from England by the name of Mummerset was expected. Feemy tried to establish—by further study of the papers—how many words would eventually be needed to make Mummerset's visit as real or believable as possible and, even perhaps, as was intimated, to make his visit central to any additional hospital procurements. The papers *themselves* already carried many wasted words.

Feemy scowled at the top paper. It was headed IMPORTANT and was signed by someone called Jane Turpin. The name was familiar to him. He underbreathed a few words to himself. Luckily they were inaudible, so were not wasted.

∞

Gregory and Suzie went through the envelopes that had arrived whilst they were away in Glistenberry; far more post than might be expected in this age of the email: mostly bills and one official-looking envelope from the National Health Service. Their respective mothers could be seen in the block's communal garden wielding clothes pegs amid raised voices that the kitchen window couldn't disguise. A mummer's play that struck the young couple as quite amusing, especially as the two women were both excessively made-up.

'What's it say?' asked Suzie.

'They're sending me to recover in a clinic near Krakow.'

'Hmmm, I've not heard of the NHS forking out for people to get better abroad!'

'I know, but there was one man visiting the hospital just before I came out—I think he was once a patient there himself—but he said he'd been on a Grand Tour of all the cities that were artistically important during the Renaissance. He went through some papers with me. But he vanished before I could read them all. Something about rigging or safety-nets. Didn't make much sense. Can't say the prospect of all those art galleries appealed to me. But I'm not turning my nose up at it. Pity you can't come with me.'

'We're not married.'

'Common law?'

'Don't think they'll pay for me. What does it say exactly?'

He starts by reading the letter aloud: 'Gregory Mummerset has been granted a place at the Yellow Valley Clinic for specialised treatment so that he can become faceless again and taken out of the limelight and put into a story that nobody reads because it is unpublished so I can be better fitted back into the humdrum working world ... and, look at this bit in the letter ... yes, reading between the lines of the new story, I'm to help pay my way in the clinic's kitchens as rehabilitation or a sort of New Deal work experience. Helping the cooks and suppliers cater for all the other patients. Oh, I get it! Our NHS doesn't pay the bill. I've got to work to earn my convalescence!' He laughed ironically. 'There's no such thing as a free lunch! Exporting ill people abroad! Not made faceless but taken off the face of the earth as far as this government is concerned! They're pretty damn clever!'

'Stupid, I say!'

'Yes. I feel faceless enough already. If it weren't for all these envelopes and my name on them...' (he fanned them out like playing-cards) '...I'd even forget my name was Mummerset!'

Gregory's share of the above dialogue (if not Suzie's) is no doubt apocryphal or merely misheard. I have little evidence that he actually thought he was in a story let alone about to be transferred to a different story. All evidence points to the fact that he simply believed he had been ill, had just returned from hospital and that his amnesia (a symptom of his illness technically known as nemophilia) had now been cured. He had just enjoyed a weekend break with his girl friend near Glastonbury Tor and was now about to be helped back into employment in his home town. However, his apparent reference to the Yellow Valley

Clinic[2] is interesting. How did he know of its existence? For that matter, how do I?

∞

The Weirdmonger perched on his wooden seat, gently touching the pulling-power for his medicine wagon with the end of his whip, as if the heat made them both lazy. The first time anyone had even considered what motivated his

---

[2] The Yellow Valley Clinic—known as the Choker when translated from the local language's rough cuts of dialect—was originally a hospital for consumptives during the Second World War. It seemed to be a strange place to site such a hospital because a self-perpetuating gentle smog or curdled mist—evidently needing no modern-day exhaust fumes to bolster it—swept along the ribboning valley from sources it has always been difficult to identify. Hence its Choker nickname. In the fifties it shook off its image, if not the gentle smog itself, by catering for more amenable illnesses than those afflicting the lungs or, even, the body generally. In other words, they began to cater for illnesses of the mind, where there was no need to have official reports about the weather conditions including the breathability of the air in the gardens. They just needed patients and doctors—and the rest seemed to take care of itself. An ideal front. There was a plaque on the gateway's structured left support—a drawbridge-type operation disguised as a door dovetailed into the castellated edifice itself that had seen more bellicose days than even those of the Second World War—and this plaque honoured a local freedom-fighter hero who had lived many more years than mortality would usually allow, a life with several names, the most famous name of which was Yellowish Haze. At the time of Gregory's period of internment in the clinic, he was overdue for this character's next appearance in the homeland's cyclic *challenge-and-response*, hence this simple observation as to his existence, if not to his complete history, as a footnote within a footnote. Regarding the clinic's own claim to have spa facilities, it is indeed a legend that I cannot currently address for lack of space or, more vitally, because of the availability of the requisite words without adversely affecting further necessary procurements by the narrative hospital itself.

wagon and, equally, the first time we've been granted a glimpse of the scrawniest steed that could possibly exist and still be able to pull a wagon or absorb words enough to give any expression of its appearance in the shape of a living creature, as if all its meat had been given away to the poor and any spare words squirrelled away for describing it now surrendered to worthier narrative causes. It snorted as each weirdmonger-wheel toppled clumsily—with timbered creaks—from hillock to hillock in the dry hustling sounds of the insidiously hot sunless winds.

The continental shifts of history reterritorialised his route across the European seas, turning them into a burnt land-mass, one that had succumbed to the global wars of warming—thus providing a logistical ability to transport by wagon his wares of rudery from Wagger Market on the outskirts of far-off Glistenberry in Summerset towards the Middle European zones of heretofore ... all carpeted by a beige desert reflecting the tender twilit skies, skies that gave off an intense heat in contrast to the intrinsic cool look of pinkness that filled the air between the arch of their horizons. Yet this was not so. Words enough to maintain the fraud are not available. But humour him. Let him wander in his imagination in natural default. Sometimes not having the right words (or any words at all) makes things seem more real.

He saw a distant disturbed duststorm churning into a section of greyed-out pinkness. He spotted the blotchy ink of rorschach shapes within its moving weather-systems, betokening a racing stampede of cattle, a situation that often faced Rowdy Yates and Gil Favor in the once popular and prime-time black and white 'Rawhide'.

'Get those dogies moving!'

The Weirdmonger laughed at his own sudden outburst of song. Then upon another horizon he discerned an indeterminate vehicle—even less focussed than his own medicine wagon—carrying what he imagined to be Gregory and Suzie towards Krakow. But why Suzie? She was not expected at the Clinic. She would likely not be allowed to enter it. Maybe her mother—with different narrative motives—had insisted that she should accompany Gregory, although Gregory's mother (or even Gregory himself) had bigger motives since any motives concerning money were always big motives. In fact, Gregory and Suzie had both sensibly agreed that she would not accompany him. But against all the odds—buttressed by love—they had set off together, tears streaking their faces, intent on saying farewell, as if she had boarded a train to kiss the departing loved one as he set off on his journey but staying on the train when the whistle went for the train's own departure. Or in denial that the train would ever leave.

Their eyes weltered as the couple crossed the arduous deserts of the Weirdmonger's imagination. They kissed each other and pined. They were now fast coming to the conclusion (in their heart of hearts) that it was too late for Suzie to disembark separately from upon whatever they had both earlier embarked. Yet they knew (in an even deeper heart) that she must disembark.

The Weirdmonger returned to consideration of the weather-systems of his newly word-populated plains of continental shift. There were many freedom-fighters in the war—a war that had beset and would continue to beset this region—some of them still alive in fact, others simply alive in history books, a few even yet to be born but already decked out in their legendary paraphernalia at the point of impending birth. Most were called after weather-systems, as if such names were imbued with more than just humanity. It was that a single dust mote in a duststorm could be a hero. A telling maxim worthy of any cause. It was also that natural motion and alternating visibility / invisibility and elementary permeability and drenched dews and muggy evenings and the ballooning-air that came at unseen, unfelt moments of the night and conscious dusks that knew it was dusk or called dusk by others and mellow mists and drained skies and red-tinged dawns and yellowish hazes and purply twilights and the hidden monsters of fogs and many more such ambient textures of vexed climates came to personify (even anthropomorphise) those who had ambition to be freedom fighters and heroes. Those who felt steeped in destiny were rocked by its tides into a gentle waking to the cause.

 The Weirdmonger sniffed. He farted. He had bad wind.

∞

When Gregory arrived at the Clinic—along with a red-faced Suzie on his arm hoping the ground would swallow her rather than face accusations of seeking free admission on his coattails—they were both surprised to see that they would need to report to Reception, then to wait patiently on a wooden bench in a waiting-room decked with tasteless paintings and peppered with light reading in the form of stale *Hellos* or *OKs*. He thought he would have been welcomed and ceremoniously shown to his en-suite room overlooking the steaming lake. This was worse than being an Out Patient. Suzie grasped his hand as she explored the lacklustre photographs of mini-celebrities in squalid pose.

 When in waiting-rooms, it is a common anxiety that the official at Reception has not noted your arrival correctly in accordance with any system of waiting-in-turn and that patients are being seen before you, even though their appointments are scheduled later than your own. This included a feeling that other people were looking through you rather than, at least, round you. Gregory suffered this concern (technically known as nemophobia) to such an extent that he frequently asked for evidence that he was in his correct position in the 'queue', forcing any receptionist to keep renewing acknowledgement of his existence.

Today, he had been informed, there would be an unfortunate delay. A man had been brought in on a stretcher, suffering from injuries as a result of a duel. An emergency, no doubt, but Suzie, after Gregory had told her about the latest excuse for ignoring his presence, said that duellists shouldn't be treated on the National Health Service.

∞

When the train pulled into the station at Yellow Valley, the medicine wagon could just be seen on the brow of one of the higher rising riverbanks overlooking the castellated edifice by the steaming lake. Whether the occupant of the wagon could see the alighting passengers of the train as clearly as they could see him, it remains doubtful—particularly as one of the endemic hazes was even then interposing a veil, doubled upon by the fumes of the halting, then shunting, train. Proustian in colour woven with the flowering of dyed cattleyas.

However, earlier, the air had been clearer and nobody could have missed seeing the very long stretcher being carried by a blonde-haired lady and a man with a black rosette through the rarely lifted drawbridge-door.

∞

Feemy had been relieved of kitchen duties to lend a hand in theatre. He was not aware of the earlier repercussions of the injured man's arrival or the nature or context of his 'accident' or the companions who had been involved in whatever had happened. He now watched further acts of unrehearsed surgery—his own hands full of something slimy that was still being uncoiled from the man's mouth—and wondered if this thing was about to be excised as a separate living creature and, if so, whether it would be given up to the clinic kitchens for a subsequent word-processing as a recipe supplementary to the ingredients of Feemy's own decreaturefication. Wordtongue soup, no doubt, this evening for all inmates—or perhaps plenty of material simply to be frozen for later use.

∞

The soft plash of oars as the dinghy floated across the steaming lake, its occupants sporadically glimpsing the Choker's castellated shape in the yellow gloom. Modal Morales and his right-hand girl Jane were searching for any face that floated upside down in the murky waters, making any recognition impossible to predict because of the wrinkled weathering by water or, indeed, the murkiness itself. They had already delivered one tall man with an untamed tongue to the Choker, but he wasn't the only one dead or nearly-dead or nearly-alive—with untamed tongues or tentacular languages that observed no traditions of meaning—whom they needed to round up or trawl for the Choker. There were 6000 of them at the last over-exact count (i.e. another 5999), each a live body or corpse or zombie representing a 1000 others within itself like Russian Dolls in layers upon layers of thickened warhide or rind formed from hardened flesh, all previously gassed by the yellow steam given off by the lake, because they (when previously normal people) had not been given the antidote to prevent such toxic intake by the lungs. Consumption upon consumption in complication of or interference by Bird Flew. The Choker sure had its work cut out for the foreseeable future.

Suddenly the dinghy grounded to a halt upon a mass of such bodies, many bony and thin (belying the scope of their contents, mental or physical), elongated in height by the torture they had suffered at the hands of history. They were intertwined like fleshy rush-mats from shore to shore. Some moaned, others weltered noisily with mud upon their whipping tongues, a few as silent as the previous silence broken only by plashing oars and the wet raw planky vessel itself. Modal, knew deep within himself, that this was a dream. He was the Clown of Dreams, and within certain layers of these dreams-within-dreams or dreams by other dreamers infiltrating his own dreams, his job was to lighten and entertain the audience of co-dreamers with antics of farce or black humour, cart-wheeling in his baggy suit through false doors to baths of custard or slews of porridge beneath his huge skidding banana-feet—all a front or subterfuge, when he reached the bottom dream or the head-lease dream, for him being the reincarnation (or actual equivalence) of Yellowish Haze himself now set to put right the wrongs of centuries, including all those killed by history rather than by natural death.

∞

Gregory was separated from Suzie at some point between his own separate dreams. He found himself waking time and time again from an operation on his head (he felt fingers manipulating his brain) as he glassily stared up at faces that floated in the yellow gloom of the theatre. This was not the convalescence he had expected. Not the lazy afternoons in a wicker chair by the side of the lake to which he had looked forward, being waited on hand on foot with all manner of medicinal cocktails. This was deep-rooted surgery itself. The convalescence, in hindsight, had been conducted at the previous hospital ward back home, a pre-illness convalescence, as it turned out, as he had then not been ill at all before then. Rest and care and recuperation and, yes, convalescence, prior to the disease hitting him. A vital pre-cursor (or pre-cure) to an illness that was incurable. It should always have been such with incurable illnesses.

Because most incurable illnesses lead to death, with no subsequent chance of convalescence. So best to have it first.

He fell back into dream. This was an anaesthetic of most confused proportions. He saw himself again as Baby Tuckoo, now a little older, a toddler with a new toy. A toy electric-shaver which, when he rubbed its business end up and down his cheeks and between his nose and lips and his chin (as a grown-up man would do with a real electric-shaver), played music.

∞

The Weirdmonger backed up his wagon (amid the alert of reverse hooting) towards the Choker's drawbridge-door. Eventually, one of the Choker's flunkeys carrying a slimy eel-like mass of rudery in his arms came out of a side door and loaded it on the wagon. The Weirdmonger gently touched the wagon's scrawny steed with the end of his whip and trundled off, having paid cost-price (with some means of illegal tender to the flunkey) for this new stock-in-trade. Glistenberry Fair was his next stop.

∞

The yellow gloom in the theatre is a sign of disease, i.e. the sepia prints of yesteryear forced through on the back of inflamed or marinated skins of passing time normally not perceptible except for this very inflammation or jaundice. Regarding the nature of the disease, it is not commonly known that places, houses, rooms etc. suffer from their own non-human form of nemophobia or nemophilia, and in this non-human form, indeed, the difference between the two complaints is even narrower than in the human form. Whether dream sickness is one of the symptoms of either or both, it is impossible to tell unless one believes the evidence of ghosts that *only* haunt the 'area' in question, if evidence can be obtained from them and, if so, whether the evidence is worth obtaining in the first place. It is thought that it was once recorded by DF Lewis in one of his long-lost books (lost because it was never a book in the first place but merely a temporary website) that Padgett Weggs (the original character that appeared in the first listed publication of DF Lewis) often listened to the droning of wartime bombers from Middle Europe as they approached the skies above London's St Paul's Cathedral (a frightening experience to those who had not seen the later cinema films depicting such frightening experiences). He would seek shelter in various underground facilities set up for the purpose, deliberately dug to interfere with real danger by the interposition of surrogate forms of assumed safety, thus releasing the disease more easily to future places, i.e. from the drains and sewers constructed by earlier Victorian engineers: pipe-systems that were now on their last legs and more dangerous to approach than actually sitting outside above ground on the pavements when the bomber planes replaced their threatening distant droning with themselves in full-bodied noise-in-vision. And the danger of disease from these ancient pot-holes of human effluence later infected the real utility living-rooms of the Fifties England (where DF Lewis spent his childhood), and steeped the public baths in melted rust by allowing dyed water to stain the dirty bodies with worse dirt than that they were trying to scrub off the bodies together with acts of public philanthropy by provision of libraries despite only being able to stock deeply foxed books and no carrels ... until history (as formulated by cinema and, later, by TV) turned a blind eye to these figuratively derelict forms of architecture whereby such places and buildings and rooms soon became just raw material for creative art by rebuilding civilisation as a fiction or, at best, a dream, all subject to implosion or disease, with wild tendencies towards non-existence at the end of the sentence which seemed to contradict any such existence by the buildings etc. at the beginning of the very same sentence. A circus of wild wordplay.

∞

Modal Morales, sipping his morning tea, thought of his mother.

Today, he wasn't the Clown of Dreams; he was back as the man everyone else thought so ordinary when he wasn't seen dreaming the day away—and they had no clue of his other life in a reality that was more real than reality itself by means of a New Magic, dreams being only just one of many methods (both spontaneous and deliberate) by which such magic could happen. He was now simply the man who ran the corner shop, handed out the early morning papers to the delivery boys and kept his business open late because otherwise he couldn't make ends meet.

Whether he himself knew he was the Clown of Dreams became doubtful even to him. But I'm sure he knew even at some superficial level that he was the Clown of Dreams but he probably had no inkling whatsoever of an even deeper level where the Clown of Dreams could make the air turn yellow in sepia backdrops of pastness with warplanes appearing bigger and baggier than jumbo-jets: old propellered flights of fighters from the Nineteen Forties but with their wings almost stretching from horizon to horizon amid sudden noises-in-vision chasing the noumenon towards the brow of the impossible made possible simply by using the words themselves. Making anything floppier or simply bigger than its proper size seemed to be among the funniest ways for any clown to make people laugh and, by laughing, believe. He sensed that this Proustian slapstick caused the massed ranks of memories to well up from the slightest trigger of tea-tasting.

By thinking of his mother, he laughed at her funny ways. She frequently said history was full of people named someone the something or someone of something, and she proceeded to speak out her list of Henry the Eighth, Hereward the Wake, Eleanor of Aquitaine, Joan of Arc, Ethelred the Unready ... Yellowish the Haze.

His mother gigglingly added the last one (after the whole series of more familiar historical names) as a sort of mother-and-son private joke but, like most nonsensical nursery rhymes, the reference had no obvious meaning, other than its custom and comfort of usage in those far-off days of his infancy when any memory was ever within his power because he could capture all the memories at once whilst, now, in tawdry middle age, there were too many memories even for the biggest possible butterfly-net to capture.

He told his mother that he loved her more than 'all the money in the world plus sixpence'.

As part of that era of custom and comfort, she had her washdays each and every Monday when the wind was always, it seemed, blowing harder and drier than on the other days of the week. Blousey Mondays with white clouds skimming across the bluest sky of all. Strange how the colour blue ever seemed associated with brilliant whiteness as in the tablets of blueness one put into the washing-copper as the sheets were boiling. His mother, if she had lived in a different age with better educational opportunities, would have been a scholar, but she never understood she was a scholar, because she was never educated enough even to have such self-awareness. And, with this instinctive intelligence and in the tradition of the historic characters named in her earlier list, she went on to name her various washing implements as Penny the Copper, Mary of Mangle, William of Washing-Line, Sidney the Suds, Albert the Clothes-Horse etc.

Modal often asked her why she did this and she replied: 'Because they are part of honesty and tradition, stretching back centuries into our country's history. You should be proud of the clean-living working-classes you come from and the well-scrubbed habits I know you will carry on into the future when I'm dead and gone.'

Little did his mother realise that, later, the world would be full of dirt both in fact and thought, with even nice respectable people swearing with four-letter words plus road rage and low TV thresholds and diseases caught *in* hospital (rather than before) ... and, indeed, the hospital staff's uniforms were so crisp and clean and well-starched, back then in his Mother's day, and this was taken for granted. But not now.

The history books themselves had grown tarnished with mistruth as infected by the rather glib lies of the modern media about more immediate happenings ... and thoughts as well as deeds have now become increasingly unclean. He was glad she had died when she had died, not even knowing about TV programmes like 'Big Brother'.

He asked her once why she didn't have a proud 'historic' name for the wooden clothes-pegs with which she fixed the rigging of the washing-line beneath the sailing clouds each Monday. She stared at her son as she considered his question ... and she cried. Somehow he knew she was thinking of his Dad, the man she had deeply loved for many years until he died. But the Clown of Dreams still never worked out why his mother never gave each clothes-peg a proper name as she did with every other washing implement. He found it inexplicably sad. I find it simply inexplicable.

∞

Modal Morales had roots—he knew—in Spain, but the family had been in the UK for well over two centuries, and he wondered how or why an arrival in England by a Spanish family could have occurred as a feasible event all that time ago, and no amount of research, he discovered, could focus on the root cause of the event but merely on its fact. He knew little of history and even less about geography. And geneaology was not even a word on the tip of his tongue.

His family had been subsumed by the local culture long before his own mother was born, and the only signs of these Spanish roots was when she failed to prevent herself cursing mildly in a form of spontaneous Spanish—with only vague resemblances to actual Spanish—as she struggled over the weekly wash. She even tried to hide her roots by studying English history and pretending she had roots there instead. The motivation was unclear. But her son failed to follow her example into such interests of local colour other than, perhaps, simply by remembering the names of real and fictional personages from history that she used as incantations or nursery rhymes to help him into an afternoon nap for a tired-out toddler.

She had died an anonymous Englishwoman with a strange name. A simple soul with strong standards of right and wrong. One who wielded spells without realising it. Serious-minded but, at a deeper level, with a place in her soul where a joke resided, a joke she never succeeded in exorcising or in even becoming fully aware that she actually needed to exorcise it. The punch line was misheard, at best.

His own looks favoured her looks rather than his dear old Dad's. Modal Morales had her snub nose, her sallow complexion at the same time as appearing as if his skin had been tinged earlier by darker pigments that had since vanished. He had her seriousness, her apparent uprightness, whilst the joke had transferred to him, upon her death, but the difference was that he knew he had to exorcise it. Masquerading as a corner shop proprietor with the deep sense of a Protestant work ethic, he patiently awaited the day 'when the circus arrived in town'—an expression his Dad had used, not his mother, an expression Modal never understood, but it seemed right and appropriate for life and its inevitable shortening by death. He guessed, too, that his Dad never understood the expression but Modal hoped that when the circus indeed arrived—for both his parents—they were given positions or performances suited to their needs. He hoped, for example, that his mother was not simply reduced to washing the clowns' costumes but, if she'd preferred, been allowed also a trapeze-trick of her own in the airy heights of the Big Top. And his Dad a custard pie of his own. Or, at least, a ringmaster's uniform. Rather than simply sitting in his caravan alone whilst the others performed, his Dad would have made a good ringmaster. But an even better clown. He hoped.

Modal sighed, as his thoughts took flight—and then subsided back to more mundane matters—as he returned to the shop's delivery book, in which he pencilled payments and orders for the various magazines and newspapers for which he arranged house-to-house dissemination by hand. It was also a convenience store for local customers who had forgotten the odd item when shopping at the out-of-town supermarket.

Surrounded by the heady aromas of washing-powder, Blue Daz, Surf, Tide, Fairy Snow, and the neutral smells of tins with smelly foods inside. And a small Off Licence, too, which was a money-spinner, but still difficult to wring a proper living from all the time he spent serving behind the counter. He rented out DVDs. And held a small stock of CDs. Old Sixties stuff, Rolling Stones, and Pavarotti, and country-and-western compilations, a few light classical CDs although Modal preferred less light music and often wandered towards both Pink Floyd and Penderecki, mixed with modern things like Goldwrap, Keane, Snow Patrol, then Top of the Pops compilations from the eighties…

There was part of himself he did not like. A propensity towards laying traps or loosening safeguards. He had yet to address this dark interior within himself—so it would be presumptuous for us to address it prematurely. He silently mouthed the names pencilled and erased, pencilled and erased, in his delivery book, listing them internally off the page: some with their real names others with ones he had made up for them: Baby Tuckoo, Blasphemy Fitzworth, Jane Turpin, Cartwheel Crazy, Mary of Mangle, Gregory Mummerset, Sallow Haze, Suzie Milledges, Padgett Weggs… All of these had recently cancelled their paper deliveries, one or two leaving their bills unpaid. Two of those names were definitely real. Others used as subterfuges, no doubt. He laughed, and then someone came into the shop for some porridge.

∞

Rachel Milledges wished she was like her daughter Suzie. Not only young, with a world of life still above the river-line, but also still relatively unreal, fictitious, bereft of any worries because being unreal or fictitious meant you did not have a mind to contain the nemo-angsts that would later beset you once the reality began to creep in. It is a lesser known fact that all fictitious characters once set in motion—created, written about, talked about, (above all) read about—would inevitably start their first gradual transformations with tiny threads of pure physicality and even purer mentality snaking along the fictitious vacuums so skilfully put in place by the writer as potential containers for life itself, even the very DNA needed to make that life work. *However crassly written.* In fact, there is one theory that crassly written fiction more efficaciously contains the seeds of magic fiction, whereby the characters step off the page and enter the room where you are reading it. How this is managed only centuries of research would nail down. More instinctive, than artful.

Rachel, meanwhile, had a grudge. Many rumours—or interferences or interventions from the narrative hospital—

in her later stages of real life as a previous fiction character had confused and, finally, corrupted the aspects with which she earlier prided herself when still half-fiction and half-real. First a shadowy, imputedly beautiful, woman with the Mildeyes name: an author herself, one who wrote the most legendary books of both truth and fiction, quoted at either end of other writers' fictions. A proud source of wisdom and visualised as a mystic of the first water, as well as a shimmering reflection of pure womanhood in its optimum form. But optiMUM was the thin end of the wedge. She gave birth to Suzie (at first in fiction, later in real life) and the radiation back of that very act turned Rachel Mildeyes into Mrs Milledges with daily concerns of washing, cleaning and baby-bathing. She found herself friends with two other aging biddies by the name of Mrs Mummerset and Mrs Morales, who equally loved nothing better than a packet of Blue Daz. Rachel Milledges only had herself to blame.

Suzie was 'walking out with' Mrs Mummerset's son Gregory. He was a no-hoper. Still mostly fictitious, he spent most of his time wandering amid a maze of inconsistent plots, seeking a purpose for living, and finding himself simply the football not a player, pushed from pillar to post, flailing between periods of loving Suzie and being in various hospitals where Suzie did not even visit. He'd later merely find himself in danger of becoming a permanent exhibit in a Friques sideshow where bits of him would be seen to have been stretched and other bits shrunk. Never to know real life in any other form. A twisted version of some other fiction he was never meant to be.

Yet it's not set in stone. Many had escaped the Friques show and were now on the way towards fruition as living, breathing, thinking people who had taken the fiction by the scruff of the neck and walked out of it in the manner of true legends as well as truths. Weirds become Words become Warriors.

The Weirdmonger's medicine wagon could be heard trundling on its four cartwheels from the distance, bringing the harvested rudery from the Yellow Valley Clinic— tugged by the scrawny and ever-diminishing Feemy Fitzworth as the wagon's motive force. The Weirdmonger merely touched that steed with the gentling forward of the emerging fictions and truths. Rachel closed her mind, inspired by such sensitivity, as she dreamed of becoming the person she really knew herself to be. But everyone (not only her) would be chasing down the Weirdmonger and his wagon in search of these ultimate truths, hanging on his every word, and needing just a single tiny nibble upon the slimy coiled now-silent cargo called Weirdtongue and thought by many to be the elixir of life.

Gregory, she knew, had been transferred from the real Yellow Valley to the non-existent Magic Mountain and now she could leave the words to their own devices, telling (as they might) of how irrelevant his (her future son-in-law's) doings truly were. Hopefully, losing him to the vacuous crassness of some other writer's narrative interference might allow her also to lose the mum from optimum. Suzie would likely follow Gregory even into the void, she knew.

Her mobile rang. It was Gregory's mum asking if she wanted to go to Bingo.

∞

As the writer of *Weirdtongue*, I cannot help having a thrill of anticipation in following through the various characters as they either develop or decay, grow fat or thin, famous or infamous, tragic or comic, humble or proud. The fact that they are beyond my control, beyond the control of anyone, makes the prospect of the passions, the sadnesses, the joys, the neutralities, the crazinesses of those pink-parcels-with-motive-force (not just pink, but beige, brown, grey or black) far more possible to set me crying for real than the traditional approach to fiction characters and their fate which the writer's or reader's inevitable knowledge of artful control behind those characters causes to be so bland and unpithy, however skilfully written or read. Simply 'suspending' disbelief is too easy. We need to nuke it. So that we can't come back to re-test it. We just let the words fall out, along with all their crass construction into wild complications and vexed textures of text, without worrying about worrying it for more. We just know we (the writer and the reader) are its meaning and our joy is letting the words die before we do. We simply put up unengraved monuments to the words. Feemy will shrivel to nothing still shackled to the Weirdmonger's medicine wagon—and Gregory will love Suzie as she will love him, but we won't know whether they are doing it to win the 'Big Brother' game or simply because loving each other is what we wanted them to do all along, even when they were ciphers that the author couldn't flesh out because he wasn't a good enough writer to do so. The fact the writer was unable to match our aspirations with his words does seem to strengthen their love when it happens because the love has grown (against all the odds) from such barren literature.

∞

Glistenberry sat, on one side, within the shade of the Tor-on-the-Hill, and beneath the sun of an over-hot British Summer, on the other. The animal zodiac was snoozing, next to invisible … it was never awake unless in rain or cold. Indeed, only a few people believed in the landscape containing or representing an animal zodiac at all. You needed to go up in a helicopter so see it plainly. And, even then, there were doubters. And people scared of flying.

When the seasonal fairs and festivals and circuses and markets came to settle with their sails upon the ocean of green and earthy-compartmented farmland—one wondered whether that was a metaphor at all but, rather, the intrinsic truth about inward voyages to the self itself. But, even in the bright sunshine, one found thoughts turning to darker visions that went above the heads of the jollifiers and holiday-makers and music-lovers and sight-seers. Rudiments of myth and melancholy.

Today, carts and wagons and tent-carriers dotted the trunk roads towards this part of Summerset, building up in volume as the traffic cycles revealed their propensity to rhythmic jamming. Together with henge-dwellers and romanies in caravans … plus ready-made canvas conveyances that were none of these vehicles but their own very special breed of transport particular to the ethos of the Glistenberry Romance.

John Cowper Powys House was, however, a dark stone building lurking quite close to the Tor area (or as the locals called, Torus) where the scratchings of the first animal sign could be discerned in the loose contours of scrubble underfoot. An animal sign that belonged to no sane horoscope or natal chart.

It is that house to which we must later divert our attention. New, as yet unnamed, protagonists are about to open the house's shuttered gloom and take root there—not as squatters, as such, but, rather, as budding contestants in some form of race that had not yet been defined (both in margins of eligible track for racing and the race's rules). They had been given permission to camp out in the derelict, dark, damp house free of charge. In the sun of daytime, the drawbacks didn't seem to matter so much. It was only at night or in gloomy weather that the darkness, dampness and dereliction crept back. A 'Big Brother' house with no audience or other ways of spying on them … except by us.

∞

'A clown's accoutrements become more effective the bigger or baggier they are … well, after all, if they're made smaller the audience wouldn't be able to see them properly. Likewise, I wonder when words are made bigger or baggier whether they take on new dimensions of meaning or effectiveness. In John Cowper Powys House—which the inmates know in its shortened form of JCP House—the JCP Foundation, as you know, being one of those lost conglomerates of state conspiracy currently re-grouping in quarters as yet unclear to people like you who never read between the lines…'

He paused as he gazed at the back of his listener's head … the latter eventually replying:

'What do you mean? People like you?'

'No offence meant, mate. Simply is that I guess I'm the same as you. Because when I do read between the lines, I infer all the wrong things. Infer is just a shortening of interfere. Get my drift?'

'I'm afraid you're being too subtle for me. All I know is that JCP House is one of those places suffering its own form of nemo-ness. A spirit of place—a genius loci—that is wildly out of kilter with its own sense of existence. It then fears it doesn't exist and therefore needs to build a reputation, a 'bigness' (as you put it) far beyond its own reality. And the bigger it gets, the baggier it gets, the more tenuous it gets, and then it implodes or sinks like a burst zeppelin or collapsed Big Top.'

'Well, yes, that's true. But, meanwhile, how about we make the house less lugubrious? Take out the dry rot. Put in a few Christmas decorations. There's no secret that Christmas is put where it is as a defence against the gloom of deep winter.'

'An antipodal angst?' The speaker laughed at his own irony.

'It helps that you can see the Tor from some of the bedroom windows. That sort of fixes it as a place with a real environment which in turn fixes the folk who stay there. 'Fix' in the sense of fixing a painting or a bit of pottery. Or poetry. Varnishing the words forever, baking them in the kiln of the writer's mind.'

'You're getting carried away. Do you mean fiction as fixion?'

The other speaker could not visualise the words 'fiction' or 'fixion' without seeing them. He suspected his co-conversationalist was not really there, because a real speaker would have spelt out the words 'fiction' and 'fixion' for the benefit of his listener. However, he went on, ignoring the slip-up by his interlocutor:-

'Back to the words. The inmates in JCP House are at this moment inspecting the large swollen words that have been left in all the rooms for them to fathom out as a sort of 'Big Brother' game. They need to separate the limbs of each letter, unstick them so that the resultant gaps reveal the nature of each letter and eventually each word that those letters constitute. Sticky with some sort of meaningless glue or porridgy substance. Some letters even seep blood. Some need mixing around to correct the spelling. Some words smell of mildew, caked with some gunge even worse than imaginable. A few words are so bloated they hang by a tenuous thread. Tissuey flesh or distended pig-bladder. Other words become inflamed like they are gorged with pus. But they remain as words. Raging toothaches. Yet they are intrinsically words. The housemates merely have to unscrabble them, palliate them. Before the words are their own words.'

The other nodded, rather distracted. Despite his increasing scrawny state, he was pulling the medicine wagon and currently the terrain was troubling him (taking his mind off the conversation), whilst the other one, riding solitary shotgun as he was, towards Glistenberry, lightly tapped his interlocutor on the shoulder with his whip, urging him on. Soon the House itself would appear on the horizon as a counterpoint to the Tor which they could already see. The driver looked back into the depths of his wagon and checked on the state of the glistening coilings of Weirdtongue (now sprouting disease-looking berries) as it, too, underwent the vibration of travel. Perhaps they should have smoked it rather than pickled it. One never really could depend on various forms of preservation. He looked again at his scrawny steed (now fallen silent), as if that was a case in point.

∞

This relates to one of Gregory's 'lost' backstories or apocryphal dreams, whereby he saw the nurse from the original hospital ward (one of many such wards he frequented later) caring for a puffy part of a word in her lap. It looked like a large single letter, with various tiny pink-stained orifices, and Gregory eventually made out it was an E after she had painstakingly finished separating the letter's limbs from the curds that surrounded them. It started to bleat plaintively from one of the orifices. Then Gregory made out it wasn't an E but an M, the nurse having turned it 90 degrees, and now it mooed dolorously, if quietly, as an undercurrent to the sound of the air conditioning. He then saw several of the patients were fondling (with their own variety of nursing care) other letters of the same word.

∞

Modal Morales made it on to TV once in his career. It was on Children's Hour—during the black-and-white era—a programme called Crackerjack. Eamonn Andrews was the host and introduced Modal as The Queezy Spaniard (!)—a clown who guested with the more famous Mr Pastry. But not only a clown, Modal was also someone who juggled balls and did a few summary somersaults. Nothing special. I don't suppose any of the children—when they eventually grew up—remembered the rather clumsy slapstick or the black rosettes[3] down the front of Modal's baggy Andy Pandy suit. Yet very few may recall the accident that happened to one of this speciality act's sidekicks—not to Mr Pastry himself but to one of the children that were required to make the physical jokes seem real. The children were volunteers from the audience. Crackerjack always had a live audience who shouted out 'Crackerjack!' in unison whenever the word 'crackerjack' was mentioned on the stage. If there had been a better quality picture (as one can now get with high definition colour TV), any viewer would have seen Modal's foot being poked out rather unceremoniously to trip up Mr Pastry but, instead, accidentally, tripping one of the children who then fell flat on his face. It was an unrehearsed moment. And the smirk on Modal's face was also concealed by the poor quality camerawork so typical of TV in those days.

Gregor was one such child viewer at home. He never appreciated the connections involved. The child tripped up, of course, was later to become the Weirdmonger.

∞

Gregor went to sleep in his flat or his tent (he couldn't remember which), went to sleep as a man and woke up as another creature that wasn't a man. He felt bags of loose flesh all around him and an enormous tail that turned out upon looking back not to be a tail at all but the rest of his body stretching back in sizeable girths and hams, hung with a distended bludder, clumsily erected upon four unsightly limbs. Unsightly to his eyes, in any event, from their perspective of view. He opened his mouth, only to moo

---

[3] The rosettes may have been any colour like red or purple but one couldn't know for certain on black and white TV.

dolorously. The body itself did have a proper tail he could wag. He wasn't sure which muscles he was using to do this but felt to be more instinctive than deliberate. He was aware of several other creatures similar to himself lined up alongside him, all heavily shuffling upon their hooves, starting to moo ever more dolorously as they looked towards the distant Torus black-etched against the rising sun of the Summerset countryside. Both viewed and viewers limned against the rising sun of some narrative hospital's keenest, craziest doctor.

There grew some awareness that they were all lined up for a race, kept behind a starting-wire by an officious Glistenberry fair official. Gregor found the ruminants of query building up cuds of obstruction in his alimentary canal, a food-chain that was, more probably, a tenuous audit trail within a series of dreams yet telling him, incontestably, that this was no dream but frighteningly real. Frightening because he had the mind of a man not that of a cow. Frightening, too, as his man's mind gathered that he was being milked for his racing prowess in some costermongering gamble-game, one that entailed odds and money changing hands among the stallholders who were holding a cow race rather than the more traditional, yet equally illegal, cockfight. Fearing a dawn raid by animal lovers, most were eager for the start of the race. Even the cows themselves, Gregor among them, seemed keen for the thing to be got over with.

He felt that he was constructed upon an insane map of bones and physical processes without logical contours. He tried to tussle around his head to bite a bone sticking out from his underswag: a wishbone that only chickens could have. He now knew he was dreaming. It was real that he was a cow. This wishbone indicated it was fast becoming a dream of being a cow turning into a bird. But he shook his head and became again the reality of being a cow pure and simple. As the starting-wire was lifted amid a raucous hubbub of cheering and mooing.

But surely this was now becoming a dream again. Gregor saw the racing-field towards the foot of the Torus, was scattered with human babies all squawling, and some simply squelching under the feet of the leading cattle. 'Get those dogies rolling,' shouted some jokester, as the stampede continued without rhyme, reason or race. Gregor found himself trampling over Baby Tuckoo, his hooves egg-splattering its head without him seeming to have any control over what his hooves did. Or he did have such control.

∞

I lay awake. I can hardly believe such scenes went through my head. It is completely dark. I am alone, as my sleeping partner earlier possessed her own sleep quite beyond me, one that has taken her away even into silence. I hear something crawling, creeping across the bedroom carpet. A creature with the ability to scale the counterpane. It is one of those squashy letters, I guess. Or, by the sound of it, two. A puffy O and R that Greg has abandoned because they hurt him so much.

∞

'How are you, Mum?'

Suzie looked towards the old woman. Was this really her Mum? The woman sat there staring glassily with those mild eyes, eyes that were so attractive when seen in the old photographs bowling along with liveliness and love, yet now, in age, symptoms of her forgotten mind's misprints in the sand of her past. She had drawn a line in it, now she had crossed it. Suddenly aware of her daughter, or the younger woman who used to be her daughter, Mrs Milledges spoke:

'Not so bad. I can't read any more, because they took my reading-glasses away. But they get us together most days for games of Bingo. I don't mind that. But they always have TV programmes on that I can't understand.' She touched her own brow and then touched Suzie's.

'Never mind, Mum. You're going to be OK.'

Rachel nodded. She sometimes had memories of following a raucous costermonger with a cart on four wheels in the streets of London she no longer recognised. Perhaps these were the real memories and the ones she had genuinely forgotten were the false memories. She couldn't expect hospital visitors to understand, especially visitors such as this woman who kept coming winter or summer, whether invited or not. The Visitor.

'Me and Greg went to Glastonbury last weekend.'

Rachel nodded again, her mild eyes now returned to the glassy stare that made the mildness so utterly bland. Suzie continued unruffled:

'You know how we like it. We saw Goldwrap. They have such a great stage act, you know. More like a circus sometimes. They sang White Horse. Shall we put them on your MP3, Mum?'

Rachel nodded for the last time in that particular visit from Suzie. She didn't understand the MP3 player and tangled earphone-wire—the tiny thing that sent such wide-sounding music through her whole soul without touching the sides. It was a comfort at night, however, assuming she remembered to put a new battery in and recalled where her ears were.

∞

Whether senile dementia is nemophilia or nemophobia, the result is the same.

When Suzie left the hospital, after seeing her Mum, she took some time to recover her own equilibrium. She popped into her local corner shop only to be confronted by its proprietor. He told her that her newspaper delivery bill was owing. She mindlessly listened to his rant before settling. She was mad, not bad, she implied. She only wanted a pint of milk, today. They ended up inferred friends again. She failed to realise the connection between him and the clown who had performed with Goldwrap the weekend before. The connection was that there was no connection at all which gave any thought that he might have had such a connection very strange indeed: and strangeness is strangely (in itself) the strangest connector of all. Establishing a connection by needing to say there was no such connection.

Greg was still asleep when she got back to the flat.

'Don't bother to get up,' she called sarcastically.

No reply. She shrugged. No connection, there, either!

∞

Feemy Fitzworth examined his own hand. It was certainly smaller than he remembered it but, literally while he thought about it, the hand's margins seemed to grow again with further inches of itself reconstituting even as he watched the process. A peculiar feeling for Feemy to feel. He had recently grown smaller and smaller, scrawnier and scrawnier, ever since dragging his body back towards England from Poland. Indeed, earlier, during transit, there had grown hazy yellow borders replacing the outer limits of his body—then vanished into thin air—then grew again as they replaced the new more inner outer-limits, leaving only bits to wrinkle and harden like stale food. Today the process seemed to be in reverse again—new areas of body replacing new areas of yellow haze. He couldn't account for such a reversal of a reversal of his body margins. And which was the direction of emaciation, and which the direction of fattening, became as inscrutable as the difference between nemophilia and nemophobia.

He should have taken the opportunity to ring his latest lady friend—Mrs Mummerset—because, soon, in fact in the last few lines of the previous paragraph, his fingers had grown too big to manipulate the holes in his mobile's tiny dial. He wanted to reassure her about a few things including his continued love for her and to establish whether he could extend the various investments she had made in his business venture as well as in his very state of existence. Words were more important than money. Even words sent via mouthpieces rather than mouths.

Later, in what he saw as moments of greater clarity, he continued his trek across the desert between Middle Europe and the white cliffs of England. He watched the ever-widening motor-kites heading to bomb some of the remaining cities that had survived Hitler's first bombardment. He felt he was being dragged down by more than just his own bodyweight. He imagined he had grown a huge tail that was leaving a deep slimy trench in his wake and that some telephony company would probably take the opportunity to lay a land-line along it in due course. He had left a charged-up webcam at one point in the desert pointing at his proposed onward route, a webcam with a connection to the tiny screen of his mobile, whereby he could now see himself progressing into the distance until his body eventually disappeared.

∞

I woke up at the sound of her voice.

'Why did you just wake me?' I asked.

'But you spoke first!'

I couldn't see her in the dark. I felt huge pouting or pulsing things on my face, things I couldn't differentiate from the skin of my face beneath them. They were a 'Why did you just wake me?' monster in bits and as a whole—its interrogative hook actually now buried in my face. But what had it said first—to wake my wife?

∞

The inmates of JCP House were still mostly asleep when the erratic alarm started to wake them one by one. They all slept in the same dormitory; they managed to get along with each other despite the rather spartan living-conditions. The place seemed ages old with no damp-courses and only running water at certain times of the day. Although surrounded by countryside, they were near enough to the nearest town to have expected much better facilities. But they were handily situated for the various entertainments that passed through the area occupying the configured fields beneath the Tor. The various Circuses or Fairs or Festivals rather serendipitously wandered throughout the land, all arriving at this particular cross-section of place at one point or other during the year and never simultaneously. That immaculate timing was a miracle in times gone by. Not so miraculous, however, today, with the availability of mobiles. A ringtone reality that not even 'travellers' could avoid. Or maybe they would have arrived unsimultaneously whatever the means of communication? Books were not written about this nor was there any wider-spread information via the news agencies, and hearsay was, of course, heretic.

The occupation of the housemates—when not attending the entertainments—was the cataloguing of books for later research by others in different parts of the JCP Foundation. But not only cataloguing. They repaired the spines and bindings and stitching and varnished some ill-finished books and restored pages that had suffered deep foxing. It was even rumoured that a few of the specialised housemates were given authority to *alter* some of the books. An overarching rule prevailed, however, that none of them were allowed to *read* the books, not even the specialists who could alter them. Anyone caught reading one of the books was inevitably punished. And one would have to resort to hearsay to establish the nature of that punishment. Alteration was therefore tantamount to faith.

The research itself into the books thus processed at JCP House took place elsewhere. Even these researchers themselves were not allowed to read the books from cover to cover. Each was given only a part of each book to read. The system of which-part-was-to-be-read-by-whom rose in a pecking-order or hierarchy of decision-making. But that is another story. Elsewhere.

The inmates at JCP House yawned as they each gradually reduced the level of the strident alarm when leaving their beds one by one. It was therefore in their interests to wake and rise as gracefully and quickly as possible, despite the propensity to be grumpy and sluggish. Gracefulness and good will seemed to reduce the level of the alarm in itself even before rising from the bed.

It was difficult to keep relationships secret in JCP House. Such close-quartered living conditions made things rather claustrophobic and the intermittent allowed visits ('holidays' was not a word allowed on any lips nor any of its synonyms) to the various outdoor entertainments hardly lifted the pressure-pot. One couple considered to be an 'item' called A and B (for ease of reference) were characters where, for once, it was not coincidental that they resembled real people. They were real people. It *was* coincidental, however, that they resembled a pair of fictitious characters called Greg and Suzie. The only difference between 'A & B' and 'Greg & Suzie' was that the former were real people and the latter fictitious. It made their love none the less, however. In either case.

A and B (resemblances to Greg and Suzie respectively) often used the same carrel within the house—a makeshift alcove combining an ancient chimney-corner and a draught-excluder papered with rather garish birdlife, preening themselves by depiction as well as by torn paper in place of feathers. The floors were carpeted plain beige, ill-tufted by wear from decades of housemates acting as cataloguers and traipsing with armfuls of books from source to study. Even centuries.

The source of books was refilled piecemeal by old-fashioned carts that doubled as provisioners for the kitchen which the housemates took turns to man. The same carts also took away the slurry. The housemates grew accustomed to the faces of the carters: garrulously grizzled countrymen in the main, interspersed with unsociable youths sporting precocious beginnings of tussocky beard growth that was dusted by the hot hustling winds in summer or given a seasonal icing come the cold winters so prevalent in the Torus area. The latter carters often doubled as supporting acts during the Glistenberry Festival. The former as roadies.

One day (during a long stint of 'cataloguing' from which memory had effaced any known beginnings) A turned to a page—ready to take authority over a proposed alteration. He knew when it was alteration day rather than simple itemising day. The morning had started with a treat: porridge laced with jam. Followed by ring-sausages upon a bed of ox tongue. A special day. But not special enough for pancakes drizzled with molasses by which *really* special days were portended. Still special enough to use an altering pen, however.

He smiled at B who shared the same carrel. She had guessed, too, this was a special day. The pancakes were missing because the carter in question had forgotten to bring the ingredients. The pancakes' absence, she assured A, did not necessarily exclude this being a *really* special day. He laughed at her naivety.

They took a surreptitious kiss that the carrel was sufficiently private to conceal from the others. But then it happened. Inadvertently, A *read* a paragraph, instead of simply altering it.

The nurse plucks my fingers from the bowl of book, teasing the letters n-e-m-o-p-h-i-l-e back upon the slowly reconstituting leaves and then leaving them outside to dry into w-e-i-r-d-t-o-n-g-u-e. The frontispiece was never discovered as I had swallowed it. They always said I had swallowed the dictionary. Wordiness and worry, they were my fate. Maybe that was the cause of my ambivalent health. A mixed blessing, if being full of words meant one could dream with the requisite words that one was empty of them.

He did not read it just like that—from beginning to end—but piecemeal, as his courage coupled with curiosity grew. Whether he absorbed all its sense is doubtful. Even a straight reading would not have unlocked the whole sense. In fact part of him suspected it didn't make any sense *whichever* way one read it.

He compounded his culpability by showing it to B who—by a gullible instinct too sudden to prevent—read the whole paragraph from beginning to end, not even piecemeal as A had done. She was shocked by her own action and stared guiltily at A. Then accusingly at him as if he had led her astray. How could he have done it? Even love couldn't forgive what had just happened.

'Why did you do that?' she asked, trying to regather some semblance of self-possession.

And then they knew what their punishment surely was—as her words flew bodily from her mouth to his face where, initially, the interrogative hook buried itself into his skull: heat-seeking then homing in on the soft-bellied brain. He did not dare to reply to B's question, in case his own words would attack her in the same way as her words had attacked him. The pain was redoubled by the fact that A and B were real people. He screeched in pain. And the voiced pain itself formed into a word contained within its own sac or cartoon bubble and flew like a vicious wasp towards B, emerging from its chrysalis at the exact moment of impact. The very words that had constituted the passage that had been read or misread in the book also summoned up their own letters' sinews for attack—initially restrained, thankfully, by the varnish that another housemate (during earlier cataloguing and repair) had applied lightly to the face of the page where those words appeared.

Before the repercussions of repeated ricochet by attacking words could become established, A and B were quickly separated by some other housemates who had gathered what was happening and hustled to different parts of the house for dewording. Sadly, such a process of brainwashing made things whiter than white and less prone to love. Such enforcements became unreversable thoughtlessness as all thoughts were necessarily prefigured by words. A and B were later that very special day summarily evicted from the house by Mary of Mangle herself and sent their separate ways back to the fictitious life of concocted characters that resembled them but were *not* them. Never meant to meet again, even in fiction. They couldn't even mourn the loss of their earlier deeply loving thoughtfulness for each other. To have loved and lost it is one form of sadness. To have never loved at all was sadness beyond measure.

∞

The seasons turned in diurnal shift and—at the perfect syncromesh of its own separate cycle—Wagger Market returned beneath Summerset skies with renewed vigour of sales pitch and costermonger's cry.

Mary of Mangle herself was today gracing its stalls with her presence—owner as she was of the farmland beneath the Tor where the Market took place as well as an important representative of the JCP Foundation. She was a tall woman—even taller than the now legendary Captain Bintiff—and walked with a gait that demonstrated her command of the lesser mortals she saw as inhabiting the bodies milling about the Market—few as tall as her, certainly none as attractive. If there was an archetypal handsome woman, it was Mary of Mangle, despite the habitual ugly wringing of her hands in tune with the 'Mangle' mantle.

Mangle, in truth, was a geographical area, whence Mary's family derived, more in common with a shrunken spit of land-locked land than with the notorious instrument of torture that some said was applied (at her behest) to recalcitrant workers on her estate (and within its houses). The uncharacteristically kinder 'arm-twisting' of their smalls on wash-day—until the last dreg or sud or suspicion of prior endrenchment had been finally squeezed out from their state as over-used next-to-the-groin sanitaries later turned into whiter-than-white tent-sails upon the Glistenberry clothes-horses—was generally considered to be a rumour.

She moved imperiously amid the Market after making ceremonial inspections of a few stalls alternately hand-picked by a retinue of flunkeys and an entourage of sycophants. It would be convenient to report that she was taken to inspect the Weirdmonger's stall itself—he being a regular of Wagger Market for many years with his displays of old-fashioned ruderies. It would have squared the circle, had this been the case, which it wasn't.

The Weirdmonger himself—the child who had once been tripped up by a clown on ancient live black & white TV—was still nursing the hurt caused by such an event. He'd track down that evil clown come what may. Little did he know that he regularly met the clown in such passages of the past that made a circus of time. One day, recognition would finally dawn. Meanwhile he demonstrated his ruderies, particularly a new speciality: a huge coiled pyramid of slimy intestines that had once been the tongue that funnelled the increasingly brown food downward and thus gave the intestines their raison d'etre as intestines although they were intrinsically the tongue itself before it turned itself (or disguised itself?) as the very intestines it fed. A throughput tongue. A very weird one. Cherished as a delicacy by those who were indelicate enough to cherish it. Offered by the pound as choice cutlets in rhino-gomenol scented wrappers—as this method of business would create more revenue than a bulk sale.

Meanwhile, G, lately evicted from Mary the Mangle's employment, wandered incognito among the stalls and sideshows. There was one bannered 'Friques'. He walked straight in as this reminded him of someone he once loved. But him being incognito, so would she be, he feared. Nemonymity as a method of loving unrequitedly.

Inside, G made out a few garbled pictures of reality which he decided to avoid as they appeared nearer a truth he couldn't yet face.

'Hey, we soon be shutting,' said a man in a rawhide hat.

'I know. What should I see if it's the only thing I have time to see?' asked G, with a glance towards the man in a moment of despising a living creature who was neither very nice to look at nor, at the same time, sufficiently unattractive to be displayed as a 'frique'. The worst of all worlds.

'The Tableau of People,' he answered without hesitation, pointing towards a stage-lit enclosure.

From his current position, G could see the back view of a family of ordinary people (not 'friques' at all, apparently). They were sitting in chairs, some leaning forward, some leaning back, of all ages, looking at another show beyond themselves that G couldn't see from where he was standing. This tableau reminded G of when he was a child and taken by his Mum to a Waxworks Museum. He was young enough to believe that the Waxworks were alive. He was convinced—by an earlier premature deja-vu of a falsely recurring dream—that the tableau family would be alive. But at heart he knew they had never been alive. He told his Mum not to worry. He thought she might be worried they were alive. But what were they supposed to be looking at? They had sat in their state of statues for many years. He went to look at them frontward. Tentatively picking his way behind the display so he could see their faces. The ultimate shock was one of the mannequins almost imperceptibly looking up at him as if to prove he was wrong, always had been wrong, always would be wrong, whatever care he put into his thoughts and preparations. He could not explain why this was as shocking as it actually was. A mixture of memory and current reality. A dread outweighing a hope. He was sure they were not real people. There is no way the feeling could be reproduced in deed or word. He left the Frique Show as it shut. Outside the tent, G wasn't sure why he had strings tagged to the top of his head and to the ends of his limbs, strings that stretched towards the somersaulting sky.

∞

Suzie wandered around Wagger Market seeking the man she didn't know she had lost. The deep emptiness in her heart, however, was concealed or disguised by a more forward feeling of adventure and wonder as she tried to regain her own footing within a new existence: following the footprints in the metaphorical sand that her mother once left for her to follow amid the plenipotentiary passages of fiction. She failed to understand, however, that these prints were misprints, making it a small miracle that her mind was soon to be reborn as a ready-made full-memoried mind taken in ever new directions by the buzz of the Market's fair. The memories were hers. But whether they were the memories of the woman she used to be remains uncertain even to the highest authorities in the Narrative Hospital. There was hopefully a place in her memory-sump left vacant for the return of the man she had lost and still sought, despite having currently forgotten both the man thus sought and the seeking.

Suzie saw that one of the fair's rides was a true-to-scale model of the great ship 'Glittenburier'. Surely it could not be the real 'Glittenburier' transported like a huge item for a new maritime version of Stonehenge: dragged here from Modern Samarkand across the deserts of Europe and placed here as a memorial to its lost captain. Then, she saw it was indeed not a ride at all—like the merry-go-rounds and helter-skelters—but rather a vision—a ghost ship made manifest—a symbol—a major item like the London Eye or the London Dome or the Angel-of-the-North—something that would remain Glistenberry's visual heritage into the distant future, outweighing the Tor and the Abbey Ruins and the Chalice Well Gardens by means of some tricksy or fabricated or truly magic fiction. If it were real how then could it really be here?[4] Suzie did not question this as she watched Mary of Mangle herself being escorted along its

---

[4] FOOTNOTE THAT HAS BEEN TAMPERED WITH SINCE FIRST POSTING. APOCRYPHAL BY HINDSIGHT. Suzie had not seen earlier—although it was possible to see it all happen from the Wagger Market enclosure had she been less caught up by her own thoughts—a police raid on John Cowper Powys House, amid much hubbub of sirens (concealed by the noise of the Market's fair). The police, following a tip-off, were after extreme nemophiles and suicide-bombers, it was reported. Many were arrested, including Mary of Mangle's own second-in-command by the unlikely name of Cartwheel Crazy who was in possession of a martyrdom video. He was later found dead in his cell—killed by police brutality, he would have later denied or claimed, given whatever means of the ability to do so.

decks by her flunkeys and sycophants: and, then, as this woman stood tall and imperious near the prow, it appeared as if she were preparing herself to be cast as its painted figurehead pointing into the storms of voyage.

Suzie decided to return to this 'vision' of 'Glittenburier' when it may have resolved the mysteries of itself by either vanishing entirely or re-establishing an appearance of a fabricated fairground ride. She could not cope with its implications or with her own inferences. Best not to think at all if thoughts were dangerous.

She wandered amid the stalls, idling the moment for its own sake. She watched a stall-holder—one advertising the elixir of life packaged within rhino-gomenol drenched tissue paper—as he meticulously sliced up a huge meaty or gristly mound of volcanically spewed gut-coils to form the contents of the said packages. Not her description, but that of an unassuming interference by one with no narrative acumen. It is difficult to get the staff. But as she watched—with the speedy resumption of assumption—she heard a ghostly costermonger's chant ('Gout cat! Spout cat! Watch their whiskers sprout, cat!'): now more plaintive than when Chelly Mildeyes, Suzie's mother, first heard it amid the streets of Victorian London. The voice seemed to come from those very coils being butchered on the blood-stained trestle-wood against which Suzie soon turned her back in search of a man she knew again she must seek and of the mighty ship that would take her to him. Except Mary of Mangle seemed to have vanished and, if she had vanished, so must the ship's figurehead have vanished—and, if that, the conjoined ship itself.

But there was little time to reconcile dream with reality because the sky suddenly darkened and roared with Middle European motor-kites in search of the young evacuees they'd missed bombing in London. And the Market-goers all scuttled for shelter, taking Suzie with them amid their surge of panic.

∞

They call me Padgett Weggs. On the sidelines of thoughts yet maybe those sidelines are where the centre truly is, as TS Eliot once implied. I need to retrace the threads. Retrack the dimensions and road-maps. Re-contour the terrain. This comes with the territory of being me.

Feemy Fitzworth with his Victorian cat's meat cart, eventually became—via temporary existence as the mutant form of a centaur—the cart itself. Once the cart himself, therefore, he needed to become, in turn, the Weirdmonger's medicine wagon, a makeshift version of Feemy's own original cart, but now, again, with a motive force provided by the good offices of the Weirdmonger. Yet the Weirdmonger's original steed died from exhaustion and Feemy needed to become the steed itself whilst simultaneously pulling himself as steered by someone else. The parthenogenesis of pulling power.

My own cart, in the old days, was a stink cart, collecting the daily doings from the neighbourhood's septic tanks before sewers were invented or when those original Victorian sewers collapsed from over-use or disrepair. I once found my mother drowned in her own tankful of doings—and I still shed a tear every day for her good Christian spirit. What a way to die by her own hand. What a wasteful martyrdom. And those brown cloggings I plucked with my finger from her throat I then dried as a memorial and, even now, keep in my trusty rucksack. The Irreducibles still haunt my memory but I remain pretty much together despite dossing near St Paul's Cathedral where these semi-Lovecraftian creatures continue to hive. Late-labelled by false imaginings that they failed to exist once, so why should they exist now. Wishful thinking. Lazy thoughts.

I witnessed the London Blitz. I have many connections with the Second World War and its ghostly residue as yellow smog during the otherwise monochrome Nineteen-Fifties. Smokeless zone, now, London. And I am probably dead, given the natural span of human life. I still recall the message from those concentrations of prisoners suffering undiluted means of regretting they were ever born: tickertape or a cascading litter of letters from the prisoners in Middle Europe: being dropped by the bombers along with the bombs—as if that assuaged any guilt. Not that I could do much to help the prisoners, unless my simple thoughts were indeed the prayers I would have prayed had I believed in God. Even at this late stage in 2006, I do not give up hope that a local guerilla hero will be able to rescue those vast amounts of victims from the clouded chambers (a hero disguised as the air or the gas itself for ease of entry) and give them a good life after all. I predict we shall hear more of this before we finish. I certainly hope so. Hope for this or any other thread attempting to fulfil its dream of reality. But return to those dark days will be prohibited if the truth makes the prisoners suffer even more than they have already suffered. Horror is only containable if one imagines the worst, but then have a 'wash-day' as it were, one that pushes the dirt to a deeper level of truth's fibre or cotton-spin where few of us can reach to dredge back and re-constitute or re-tell. Not wishful thinking any more. Not lazy thoughts. I thank my mother for my own fortitude. God bless her soul. Mrs Weggs, a far greater woman than the Missues Mummerset, Morales or Milledges.

Whilst here, I should mention that two further threads will be straggling to a close whereby the Weirdmonger seeks the clown who had tripped him up on live TV in the Fifties, both now seeking symbiotic revenge and a battle below the Tor. And, also, whereby Suzie searches for her beloved G who hopefully—by this very process of being sought by his soulmate—will quickly resume his Gregness, his Gregorness, his essential Gregoriness as soon as such mutually rediscovered love (beyond the insidious trammels of Mary of Mangle) works through the fibres and cotton-spins of their own sure-fire destinies to forge a loving reality for themselves from mere fiction. Wishful thinking? We shall see. War is everpresent between the Words as well as between the Worlds and, suddenly, I fear many a slip between cup and lip as each letter lifts up from the page one by one. Soggy, puffy, blood-bloated letters: no longer the cheerful tickertape or cascaded litter…

∞

During the height of the panic caused by the unexpected air-raid over Wagger Market, Suzie found herself hustled into a surprisingly available shelter that was almost 'fit for purpose'. It was better than the ones in London—i.e. those hastily dug for the Blitz proper by means of Anderson Shelters in city-street gardens together with makeshift kip-points on Underground platforms—but, even so, it was too dark to see very clearly in this subterranean part of Summerset and the walls were still earthen without any attempt to finish them off by plastering.

Later that night Suzie was to fall asleep with difficulty creating dreams that she was sheltering, along with others, within a bodily cavity still warm from continuous life that had been fortuitously provided by one of the terrestrially in-built 'animals' of the Glistenberry Zodiac. But, whilst still awake, she was faced with harsh reality, despite the best intentions of those who had built this particular shelter.

At times, she also believed she was within a chamber that would soon be full of a deceptively pale yellowness, but she could not fathom this belief.

For a while, the shelter's inhabitants looked bleary-eyed, cowed, taciturn, rather than outright scared or at risk from suffering any renewals of noisy panic. They could all hear, no doubt, the dull thumps of bombs distantly shaking the ground. Suzie feared for the integrity of JCP House, even the pinnacled brick-built Tor stuck up high on the hill above Glistenberry for many centuries. The Abbey Ruins would be ruined even further, she thought. She also feared for the safety of someone she did not know. She ached for this very stranger's arms to enfold her.

Before finally falling asleep, she had cast glances around her co-shelterers, some now mumbling in odd twos and threes. She forced back the dreams that teetered upon the brink of sleep's approaching onset. She spotted—for real—a figure that looked remarkably like Mary of Mangle herself. It was surely, indeed, that very woman. Suzie had often seen her on regular tours of JCP House. She looked less imperious, now, less certain of herself, but still with an air of tallness despite sitting down on the rough floor. Pitiful to see such a downfall, despite the imputed cruelties of her reign.

Mary of Mangle opened her empty mouth widely meeting darkness with darkness. Some of her flunkeys and sycophants approached her. One tried to force-feed her with a large amount or tripe-like slobber that the Weirdmonger had earlier been seen (if not seen by Suzie herself) cutting up as an elixir-of-life on his Market stall. Mary of Mangle refused to swallow it but kept it in her mouth, like a spoilt child. As some of the substance was now missing, the words she eventually emitted by its means—via the curds of its thick slobber—appeared incomplete: 'Gout ... Spout ... Watch ... the ... Sprout ...!'

Others turned towards this sound of her 'voice', half-heartedly mystified. Then they returned to further attempts at sleeping, as helped by what they put down as a dream. If one was dreaming, then one must be asleep. A great psychological help towards real sleep itself.

In another corner, a rank-smelling man tossed and turned in his premature sleep, using a filthy rucksack as a pillow. Suzie thought he would have been more comfortable without the pillow. She bum-shifted away from that man as far as possible because he was now speaking of things in his sleep that she did not wish to hear together with the sound of farts she did not wish to smell. She was, consequently, nearer Mary of Mangle herself who had, apparently, fallen asleep, still ruminatively chewing the curdish cud with a renewed air of sway and swagger and pride that only the oblivion of sleep could have brought to someone so fallen from grace.

Modal Morales picked up one of the papers in his shop. There were news agency photos of a freak storm in Somerset. Glastonbury Tor had been toppled. Amongst the crowds that subsequently gathered (in one of the more detailed photos) around Glastonbury Abbey's shattered remains, Modal half-recognised a face he did not wish to recognise at all, one which gave him an inexplicable frisson of fear. He fingered the black rosette in his lapel and replaced the newspaper in the delivery boy's pile—and looked up as the shop door went 'ding'!

∞

As they were not there whilst suddenly they were there, the words *weirdmongery* and *weirdmongering*[5] came to a communicado of consciousness in almost commando

---

[5] It has been drawn to the attention of the Narrative Hospital that the letters of *weirdmongery* and *weirdmongering* will give rebirth eventually to *Gregory*. This fact means that, at hopeful best, from this novel's eschatological as well as scatological conflict, there will eventually arrive curative assistance for Suzie to locate the man she so assiduously seeks for the benefit of a happy ending.
   Or, more negatively, just a placebo for pests.
   But, at dreaded worst, just letters fucking each other.

ferocity—then subsided to a more gentle entry as the shop-door's *ding!* of awakening subsided to just an echo. These words knew they were born of the original Nemophile—participles, nouns or gerunds of being or doing that the Nemophile had remotely ignited with his very existence on the seat of his feemicart continents away. He was probably just as unaware of the process as the words were unaware of themselves, whilst being simultaneously operative of that very process by osmosis through magic fiction. Namelessness anthropomorphised as letters riding shotgun on the very word-carts they formed.

If letters or words have consciousness, it's hard to penetrate their haze. Yet we do see—via a blur of our own semantics, phonetics, graphology and potentially co-operative syntax—that a man is standing behind a shop counter, a mouth like an O of surprise ready to swallow the very pests[6] that peer in at him from the still dark pre-dawn street outside.

---

[6] These pests appeared to be a strange language of words with voices using the words as sights rather than sounds. Mr Morales did not understand exactly what he was seeing but instinctively, if with nemophiliac distraction or detachment, he sensed that this language called Weirdtongue was indeed called just that: Weirdtongue. It was a genuine world language, rather than an experimental Esperanto-like attempt to draw in all the languages of the world (except Basque or Hopi) and turn them into an easily understandable communication system upon air or paper for even the simplest of mortals and peasants to use. Esperanto had failed because it ceased to be organic or intrinsic to the meanings. Weirdtongue, on the other hand, was more a religion than a language, but serving both purposes—a religion that needed no prior understanding, because its components stuck to the skin like burrs and poured meaning via the pores into the mind without the intervention of intelligence. Religion at its worst, even if *all* known religions were similarly bad enough to a greater or smaller degree. The vexed outcome was that not only meaning was injected but also poisonous thoughts that attached to the meaning like a

The pests are something that we identify with, as words. I, as a single letter, feel my limbs are puffy, swollen beyond measure, as they thus disguise the letter of which these limbs are part and the word of which the letter is, in turn, part.

I struggle to maintain the onward purpose so easily forgotten. The Nemophile's thoughts have drifted away from us. And thus the blur remains, strengthens. Simply the O left.

Frozen in time. Until, at least, the thoughts eventually returned to revive our letters and words: encouraging us to form a retributive phalanx aswarm the clown's face like a Biblical plague. But nothing, it seemed, followed the *Simply the O left*. No words at all. Not our words at least.

∞

Suzie visited her Mum again in hospital. They touched each other's brow in tune with some tradition of tenderness that neither understood.

'How are you?' asked the erstwhile Chelly Milledges as she eye-balled the woman she no longer knew as her daughter.

'I'm fine, Mum.'

'Fun?'

Not even the words matched each other.

---

particularly virulent type of fiction. Not Horror fiction as such, but, in the same way as Classical Music was reputed to be fiction stories injected straight into the vein without the necessity of reading them first, this language of *true* fiction was black magical realism: a fundamentally weird-corrupted 'langue' that later turned into bodily cancers and tumours (euphemistically known as 'pests' in the jargon), starting with the tongue itself. Quite a drawback for any language.

As if waking to the trigger of the word she thought she had repeated, Mrs Milledges bounced up and down in her chair, a smirk from cheek to cheek.

Suzie frowned. 'I know you are not listening to me, Mum, but I feel I've lost someone I once knew. Someone special.'

Her mother nodded, still maintaining a maternal gravitas, despite the nemophiliac illness that, like the neologistic adjective itself, made life seem meaningless.

They both cried without understanding the tears. Suzie's guilt was re-doubled because, at her relatively tender age and reasonable state of health, she *should* have understood.

∞

I rarely have visitors. The hospital is kind to me. I know who I am, even if they don't. I am the voice I hear in my ears. I am the heart that beats within my breast. I am pregnant with my only daughter. It's a difficult confinement. I always have known it would be. My life will hang by a thread when she's finally born. How do I know it's a girl? I am too old-fashioned to understand how anyone knows the gender of their child before it's born. Allow me at least that miracle of failing to know something. Allow me to be old enough not to understand how you know most things that I don't.

Today I have a visitor. She calls me Mum and I wonder how that terrible tragedy of her birth has allowed her to return and visit me and call me Mum. I surely died from childbirth.

Today I have another visitor. I am more comfortable with this man although the hospital staff don't seem to realise I have a visitor at all. It is my daughter's father. He cries of cats and other things. He smells of bad meat. He smiles. I forgive him his crime. He calls me Chelly. He calls me his sweet Chelly. He reads me tongue-twisters to divert the long hours.

Today I have a nightmare. I dream of meat. Saddles of beef, sirloins and briskets, dolorous ruminants in bright red apparel. Steaks that rot on the t-bone. They tried to escape but they were caught and brought to my nightmare feast.

I have that woman who calls me 'Mum' today as a visitor. She visits more often than I wish. If she were in hospital, I would not visit her. She tells me about her dreary life. She has a boy friend and they like music. She puts something in my head and I listen. She says I will like it. Help pass the time. It is noisy. A good beat, though.

I wonder whether she sees what I see in the mirror when she looks at me. I see a huge tongue-twister in the bathroom mirror when I look. A storm of flesh set to flatten all the houses. A freak storm.

'Mum, Mum, are you there?'

I pretend not to listen. Peter Piper Picked a Peck of Pickled Pepper. I say it over and over again. Hiver, Hiver, Hiver. The noise in my ears. Something on my head, not in it.

'Mum, mum, are you there?'

I whisper this to myself when she has gone. She's my little chickadee. Sweet chickadee. I lost her when I was born. In the deep deep winter.

∞

Near the Clinic with the drawbridge door—if thoughts can go that far back with such a mist of memory as imagination has garnered from a higher power—was situated a cavernous cathedral, built far underground and made of salt crystals, scintillating and gorgeous as the deepest and whitest white: a cleaned-to-the-bone image of purity fit for the resplendent trappings of such Godly awesomeness. Acres of Heavenly wash-day even if the blue skies could not blow healthily upon these sparkling mountains of inner Mass. There was simply a buried Arctic wonder searingly bright and beautiful. All the box pews, the towering altar and the confessionals were shimmeringly stacked tight with a salt-mine's very essence. But our local hero needed somewhere to practise his art of imitating underground fumes and such a scenario was the ideal site for a dress rehearsal. He planned to disguise himself, indeed, as a toxic gas that could penetrate the evil chambers elsewhere in which millions were currently suffering: so as to rescue them. Sadly, the white cathedral was consequently stained yellow by his whirling dervishes of hissing miasma. A trial and error of necessary evil. A means that surely would be justified by the ends.

∞

A and B sat on the bank of a very wide yellowy river running between many hybrid geographies natural and man-made—amid the callow mellowness of a fly-blown late afternoon. A, his face badly word-scarred, was idly fishing in the sluggish current of the river, at its most sluggish where he fished the edge—seldom looking at his rod and line, merely hoping for a tug from the fish of all fishes, whilst knowing in his heart of hearts that such creatures frequented the deep middle of the sallow river not its tussocky margins. B watched A from her rather aloof position behind and above him.

He turned to her to speak: 'I wonder how they're getting on at JCP House, since we left?'

'I'm glad we had to leave,' she replied. 'The best of all solutions, in the end. I gather Suzie who I'm supposed to represent is still looking for you—well, I mean, looking for her loved one whose name she has forgotten who may or may not have been represented by you when in a raw state. All this, I suppose, because we were abandoned by the words after they took them away from your face, but we can't carry other people's burdens on our shoulders, can we? We have enough of our own.'

'You are too formal,' said A. 'Be more chatty. We need to appear real, otherwise we shall eventually vanish altogether. Be more colloquial when you speak.'

He laughed, absent-mindedly throwing a few fine-ground crumbs from his diminishing supply of stale bread in the hope that such powdered provender floating on the scum would attract the fishes better than an unbaited hook under it.

'Colloquial? That's not exactly a very chatty word … although I suppose it *means* being chatty!' She was now affronted.

A enjoyed chewing the fat, even if he thought that B wasn't now listening: 'I'm not sure why I tried to write it all on the internet. If I were going to write a novel, it would have been better on paper. Then go through all the right channels of marketing etc. And the words would then have had more provenance. On a screen they do not match with the theme of letters and words actually coming to life like creatures that live temporarily on paper. They're only pixels or something like that if done electronically.'

"Provenance' is not very colloquial!' interrupted B, sarcastically. 'Anyway perhaps it's safer if the words are produced electronically rather than on paper. Once they are on paper, you may not be the only one suffering from a badly word-scarred body! Every reader would suffer. I don't suppose any publisher would *dare* to put your novel on paper!'

'Yup, maybe. But, meanwhile, I've had much criticism about the *method* of what I do rather than criticism about the thing-in-itself, the noumenon of the novel…'

'Hell! You're smug!'

'I don't know. I'm just me.'

'Well, if you want criticism. Your novel stinks. It's a mishmash of themes—completely lost the plot like 'Lost' itself.'

'How can you say that? Look! I can now actually tell you that Suzie has by now reached the Magic Mountain looking for him. It was always fated that the man she seeks would eventually end up there.'

'He's not got free will, then?'

'Well, let's not get ahead of ourselves. Suzie looks through the mountain, stone by stone, then via caverns of salt crystal, in search of one thing. You know what it is?'

'Don't tell me. The letter G.'

'Could be. It's a start, at least. It will be sitting there like a bloated crab—and in the middle of the open-ended G of crustaceous bone there is yellow pus—a crab that can only live in darkness. She will blind it if she takes it back to the surface.'

'That's really sad. You *could* be a good writer if you thought things out a bit better. Flesh out the characters. Allow sadness to develop gradually, not have it up front—in your face, as it were.'

'I don't know. By the way, all themes are craftily connected with each other. Not a mishmash at all. Take Mary the Mangle for example. You, for example, are a 'tabula rasa' for Suzie and I for the man we now know simply as G. Mary of Mangle is made up of four old ladies—that's why she is so tall—Mrs Morales, Mrs Mummerset, Mrs Milledges and Mrs Weggs. All flattened together by the wringer that is contained in her name—so as to become a credible carrier for the really long Tongue itself. A carrier or connecting device to stitch the novel together. Like the novel's language itself.'

'Hmmm. I thought Weirdtongue *was* a language not a physical tongue. Or should I say tonguage?'

B laughed at what she had just said, and then laughing even more wildly as she watched A suddenly take a bite.

The thing he caught must be enormous, judging by the fight it was putting up. Flapping about wildly in the yellow scum while they tried to interpret its evolving nature as a single letter and then as a single cumulative word and finally even as a thing-with-many-words, the various swollen cells of this sudden catch connected by the adhesive of riparian cancer.

B, despite her misgivings, went to help A in the process of landing his catch: a toing and froing of vigorous tug and deceptive release upon the narrative line: a battle between man and fiction of much duration. So busy, neither A or B noticed that—upon the opposite bank of the river—a circus and all its caravans and paraphernalia was in slowly trundling transit between pitches.

∞

Mrs Celia Mummerset missed a number of people.

She still visited the living body of Mrs Rachel Milledges at the hospital whilst the real friend who used to exist within that body was missing, presumed lost forever. Mrs Mummerset also missed her own son: she knew not where or why. She kept her mobile switched on day and night in the hope he would ring—with the combined hope that her latest male admirer (another missing person) would also ring: from abroad where she believed he was currently travelling on business. She missed Mrs Lettuce Weggs who had drowned in her own septic tank. She missed another friend: Mrs Maria Morales who had died one wash-day…

The circumstances concerning this death of Mrs Morales are still *sub judice* or, at least, subject to a version of their own circumstantial evidence. Her son, Modal, one Monday morning, left his corner shop—having shut it with a card on the door saying 'back soon'. He seemed to have deterred most regular customers, in any event. He was intent, today, upon setting off to visit his Mum for some advice regarding the pests that had attacked him. She was an expert, he knew, upon old-fashioned complaints that bore names from old wives' tales and that only the old wives themselves—versed or steeped in the real past as they were—knew how to suffer properly or with dignity.

Ever since the pests—as he knew them—had attacked his shop, he had felt one such pest eating away at him from under his skin. To help palliate it, he needed simply for it to be named. His Mum was a wise woman, better than any doctor. Modal loved her in his own quaint way. In any event, he was, today, finally, at the end of his tether, having decided to shut up his shop and tell his Mum, without further delay, about his own worst fears. But he had forgotten it was wash-day. He should have guessed, however, judging by the breezy blue of the sky and the fulsome white billows of configured clouds veritably racing above him like the airy ghosts of cattle.

'Hi, Mum!' he shouted as he spotted her pegging out smalls on the washing-line. 'How's Sidney the Suds and Albert the Clothes-Horse?' he continued shouting as he thus joked across the street from where he could already see her waving at him.

Yet, from that distance, he spotted that she seemed skinnier than her habitually jolly wash-day plumpness. Now as thin as when she was a young slip of a girl during the Spanish Civil War all those decades before. The matter somehow concerned the ancient rusty-handled mangle through which she'd just been strenuously wringing the sodden clothes. Nobody could later fathom exactly the nature of any available circumstantial evidence—other than that she turned out, upon investigation, to be quite dead, waving like a flag from where she was pegged out upon her own washing-line.

∞

Years in the past, the four friends (as recently uncovered by careful research at the Narrative Hospital) had an excursion downtown—or as they call such gatherings nowadays: a 'Hen Party' where women become drunker and more raucous than the usual standards of behaviour would allow for members of the gentle sex.

Their already known names were Seely, Chelly, Lettie and Maria. The last one didn't like her name shortened—having recently arrived in the country from Spain where strict religious considerations disallowed names being tampered with. A beautiful bevy of long-legged lovelies celebrating one of their birthdays during an era of English life when it was still ostensibly monochrome (according to the newsreels) but where life was actually far more colourful than the dowdy impression passed down to observers such as the staff of the Narrative Hospital. That early era was, for example, full of dances like the Black Bottom, Jitterbug, Charleston and Jive. And promiscuous sex was rife yet covered up. The event in question here (of which we speak) was a real one. Not a concocted one as many of our researches here at the Hospital have since demonstrated other incidents to be. This 'Hen Party'—so-called—really happened. It was not and is not fiction. It has provenance undeniable by any method of trying to disprove it.

However, there is still some doubt relating to whether the four girls met up with four gentlemen during the course of the evening. The word 'gentlemen' is used for ironic purposes. They were undesirables, not to put too fine a point on it—but the girls' perceptions and normal acuity of taste were blurred by drink and revel. One 'gentleman' was called Tongue. Sporting a silver stud in his namesake within the mouth. The second: Monger. The letters 'PEST' were tattooed on his forehead. In fact all the 'gentlemen' were tattooed with various words to a greater or lesser degree, both covered and uncovered. It was just that Monger's

'PEST' was by far the most outrageously prominent. The third was called Dinnerman. He seemed to be eating away inside. The fourth: his name unclear, although, by the process of elimination, we have come up with the most likely possibility: Coco.

The group's conversation, however, is clearer (at least in part):

'Where you girls from?'

'Not too far and not too near.'

Giggling laughter.

'Do you drink hard stuff?'

'If you're paying!'

More giggles, followed by two of the girls (Maria and Lettie?) getting up to jitterbug together, just as the typical music of the London Blitz era took brassy sway ... with, later, the odd crooning song from a second-rate vocalist..

We believe it was Monger who spoke next, his eyes upon each of the two remaining seated girls in turn:

'Well, you've heard of talking fire?' His voice was mellifluous and uncannily believable, even though this was before the period when he was due to perfect his art of producing words or weirds that were undeniable truths even if they weren't.

'Talking fire?' the two girls asked in unrehearsed unison of echo. They were rather bemused, apparently, by the direction of Monger's chat-up line.

'Yes, well, fire that talks is as nothing when compared to talk itself catching fire.'

He looked meaningful as well as mean. We have failed to uncover further items of the conversations that night and the eventual repercussions of the meeting are still clouded as we have suffered a decided lack of the requisite funding here at the Narrative Hospital. Many stories have had to be abandoned through lack of assistance. We hope however that the partial stories we have managed to cover (and still intend to cover) will eventually form a configured pattern, i.e. an emerging gestalt worthy of any literary work that aspires to be a novella, as our overall experiment in 'magic fiction' surely does aspire to become, whatever the hindrance created by disinterest and by our periods of depleted confidence here at the Hospital.

∞

It was like Chinese Whispers in reverse—overhearing some whispering as each new pair overhears the words overheard by the previous pair without the necessity of repetition until reaching the first pair who overhear it all over again in puzzling counterpoint. Not even puzzling, if memory has lost the ignition of the original 'whisper' by the time it returns as a full-bodied theatrical aside. It is strange how words can seem to live without the necessity of re-articulation: becoming a living, breathing force themselves until one wonders if they need human intervention at all, passive or active.

Suzie returned to Glistenberry and was amazed how the spirit of the place—its *genius loci*—had changed since the frique storm. The hill where the toppled Tor had once stood seemed somehow bigger, more mountainous, more magical. In the Abbey grounds, the ruined Ruins were somewhat sadder. Less magical, but more grindingly religious. The Chalice Well Gardens were water-logged and carried a swamp fever variant of riparian cancer—as if the Yellow River itself had threaded the European deserts with the consequent further staining of its namesake appearance from the lack of colour-fastness in the painterly sand dunes that it undulated above and below to reach these very gardens. In some quarters, yellow was a brave colour—symbolic of heroic acts. But today, in Glistenberry, Suzie was disturbed by the insidious personality the colour had gained by transit and transformation between Middle Europe and Summerset.

Despite the wonderful image of the now Torless hill as the very Magic Mountain of legend, the stripping out of the inferred animal zodiac from the surrounding fields by the storm had deterred the various fairs, festivals, markets and circuses from returning to occupy its landscape. Now an essentially tarnished landscape. Many failed to see the magic in the 'mountain', in any event. But Suzie did.

Thus, attracted by the sole residual attractiveness, that of the so-called 'magic mountain', Suzie decided to spend the day searching for G on its slopes. Even under them if she could dig far enough with her bare hands. She knew she loved G. But she'd forgotten why.

Cattle still grazed its lower slopes, but with even more dolorous mooing and lack of stamina. Their race of ruminants was well and truly over. It could be called sadness, but if one overhears the word too often it sounds like a seaside resort: sadness-on-sea ... shading away into mere sandness ... and the once hopeful spice voyages to Cathay and Samarkand now bogged down in silt. Abandoned for the sake of recrimination. Persia and Ur sinking into underground rivers of nuclear waste.

If only Suzie had known she could have avoided all the heartache of slope-scouring. G was in the name Glistenberry all the time.

∞

There was one circus that still returned to the vicinity. Not as close to the Torlessness of Glistenberry proper. But towards Wells where a cathedral still squatted despite the desecration of its views. Modal Morales was now chief clown and was never palmed off with the ringmaster's job. He still resorted to some dirty tricks—it was in his nature— like the loosening of an odd trapeze or the acidifying of the odd custard pie—but he always regretted his actions and spent lifetimes of self-denial to nurse his victims back into health. He was a walking hospital that had damaged its own patients in the first place.

He no longer wore black rosettes on his baggy Andy Pandy suit, but red ones, as he recently discovered his father Coco used to wear red rosettes when clowning was a reputable profession and you could appear on TV along with stars like Mr Pastry and Clive Dunn. Children loved clowns then.

In sight of the cathedral, the circus was climbing the sky piecemeal and crawling the ground in ill-defined maps of lost islands. Modal was not too hoity-toity to mess in and help set up the Big Top and attend to the animals' ablutions. He did not even think about what was what or who was who. He tried to switch off his mind and, with it, the recent dream sickness of losing his Mum's joyful skill in walking washing-lines. When he wasn't working, he simply watched the hazy ring-cyclists crossing the sky-line limned against the hugely setting sun either side of the louring cathedral.

The Weirdmonger—after seemingly centuries (judging by the clock in his heart) of scouring the world for the Elixir of Life—had returned to the circus as a safety-net consultant, and not its boss. Nobody now realised there was, indeed, no top authority within the circus. Very few in fact knew that the Weirdmonger was now amongst them again unless they accidentally overheard the fact. They vaguely heard it rumoured, however, that the embarrassment he had once suffered on Crackerjack was of more importance to him even than the Elixir of Life, having extended his journeys across the whole of Europe simply by the magnetic force of aspirational vengeance. But hardly anyone believed rumours.

The circus had become a leaderless commune and anarchy was just another tight-rope act.

The Weirdmonger just sat in his medicine wagon dreaming of the old days of Wagger Market and of when he spent 'centuries' rubbing thoughts into his brain via the forehead—or was that just an attempt at erasing the tattooed letters? You could still see the residual livid scar of the P and the even fainter remains of E, S and T if you looked close enough. But nobody dared.

At night you could hear Baby Tuckoo crying. Nobody rocked his cradle. Just another eraserhead.

∞

Yellowish Haze started his incredible heroic adventures in concentrated war effort by a complete pre-briefing in a hospital ward that was situated beyond the door that acted, when open, as a bridge for the stagnant moat. There he exchanged secret passwords with his linkman by the name of Simplon, masquerading as a doctor. Apparently Haze needed yet to endure many further processes to his body as if his earlier rehearsal of mere swirling around the salt-mine was nothing but child's play when compared to the real thing. However, during that previous rehearsal, he had lost a lot of body fluid in the form of sweat and urine seeping through all his skin-pores as had been evidenced by the staining of all the available surface salt configurations or sculptures in such a huge cavity underground. But now that admittedly difficult liquid process needed to become an even more difficult gaseous one.

'Not many men have the ability to turn into gas,' said Simplon with gravitas.

Haze shrugged—he was destined for this glory because of his name, no doubt. He did not query such a paradox as a name preceding what the name was not yet famous for or had not yet created the fame for itself in hindsight. Such tributes by naming usually followed a different direction. God was only called God after the event. He shrugged again. Saint Yellowish Haze. Sounded good. He now smiled.

Simplon was doggedly fingering an over-large human tongue on a plate, earlier organ-donated—as Haze had witnessed—by one of the dinnermen who worked in the hospital kitchen. It had been already been stitched with various loose ends to help manipulate it. It was not, however, a genuine Weirdtongue—as it would have to be far longer and plumper and juicier to have been a Weirdtongue. It was said that there was only one genuine Weirdtongue in the whole world and this had been smuggled from country to country disguised as a whole human being.

The tongue in Simplon's ward was of secondary weirdity. It served its purpose however as Haze's proposed transfiguration in an almost religious process of speaking in tongues. This tongue could be worked like a magical trick to split infinities when babbling and Simplon read a rather abstruse spell of summoning gas with his own tongue in counterpoint to the puppet tongue on the plate. Simplon yanked on one of the strings and the tongue jabbered loudly, using the plate as if it were a rather large tooth and Simplon's cupped hand as a distant echo-chamber or mouth. Haze was amazed how the intricacies of such a ceremony had ever been invented from scratch because each part in the process seemed to follow one unlikely event with an even unlikelier event time and time again. Growing ever beyond description or ratiocination. Only wild guesses could follow any logic in the presumably strict rotation of spell and counter-spell.

Haze watched—with increasing nemophobia—his own skin growing into an ectoplasmic gas with each tug on the tongue's tags by Simplon. How Simplon's body itself avoided the process was mysterious and, indeed, from time to time, Simplon had to burn off some of his own product of gas with a cigarette-lighter. Simplon was a lugubrious fellow with tall features and a sunken smile. He talked with a deep voice that the tiny tongue in his mouth did not seem capable of producing, even with the barrel chest available as part of Simplon's propensity to breadth as well as height. Soon all Simplon could see was Haze's namesake swirling around the room with a noxious stench that had been deliberately instilled to protect against unexpected leaks by revealing the existence of such leaks through the sense of smell. Simplon opened a valve in a dialled gasometer on the ward's wall and watched the wild ribbons of yellowness that had been Haze vanishing into the complex pipe systems that threaded the underground of wartime Europe.

'Damn! I forgot to tell him which way to go!' Simplon said to himself. Shrugging nonchalantly, he picked up the puppet tongue and commenced to munch it as a means of destroying the evidence. He instinctively picked up his mobile and rang someone abroad but whoever it was couldn't hear what he said because his mouth was full. Mrs Celia Mummerset shrugged and wondered who had called. Whoever it was had withheld their number, she noted. She wondered if it were her dear long-lost son. Or that no-good Feemy Fitzworth. Wasn't her dear friend Chelly (who was now sadly suffering nemophilia) née Fitzworth before she was Mildeyes or Milledges? Or was it Chelly's daughter Suzie? Mrs Mummerset would never understand anything. At least you can't lose a mind if you never had one in the first place! She laughed. Then shrugged. Time for her afternoon snooze: a restful dozing in counter-rhythm to a wheezing cough that threatened to rattle the prison-bars of her asthmatic chest. She'd forgotten she'd left a pan of porridge on the gas stove.

∞

It is a joy not a job. My name is not Simplon. I am *a* simplon. Employed by the JCP Foundation.

I was one of those simplons who attended the meeting in Glistenberry with Jane Turpin and others. I think, however,

I *was* directly mentioned but I'm too busy today to have a look. The links are simply too many for me to untangle them all. Some days I simply don't care. Let the inconsistencies have full reign. I work my hands to the bone, in any event. Just because I forgot some of the pre-briefing details for Haze's journey in the Nazi gas-pipes doesn't necessarily make me a bad person. Indeed mistakes make a good person, a *believable* person. And that is important when dealing with such matters as we have before us here.

So I didn't pop up simply from nowhere. My job—yes, my joy—is to simplify and iron out the wrinkles in wash-day sheets, wrinkles that seem to appear willy-nilly simply by looking at them. I am often unvexing the texture of text itself.

I correct the mistakes and that includes my own mistakes. I am no perfectionist. I simply give hindsight a fighting chance.

For example, there is some difficulty with the Fitzworth lineage and its various miscegenations. Feemy's brother Churles, where does he come in? Who really is Suzie's father. And Mildeyes, Milledges, Fitzworth, many a map makes a maze before the birds flew home.

And there is the conundrum of Padgett Weggs and Captain Bintiff. The latter was the original carrier of the Weirdtongue. That's all I know. And Weggs? Who is he? Who is he? Who *is* he?

And what happened to G's earlier ambition to be a ringmaster in a circus? And who is G? Why has he lost touch with the plot? His name's important. All our names are important. I should know. I feel so bereft without a proper one. Don't let anyone persuade you otherwise. We shouldn't let the thin edge of the nemophiliac wedge drop everything into darkness.   Grrr! I get so impatient sometimes. A simplon being simply inbuilt with various angsts and phobias. It helps with untrammelling others if you know what they're going through from personal experience.

And Feemy is becoming thinner and thinner the less time we spend using words about him. Almost like gas himself. Or the stench of decayed meat. My job is to re-summon the words about each character so that they can reclaim their own body. A delicate job, as too many words makes them fatter than they should be. A fine balance to be struck. And I'm not sure any simplon has been trained enough (or fundamentally contains the requisite potential) to make such responsible judgements. The remuneration of existence is sometimes just not enough to recompense us! Stress is counter-productive. I wanted to make my position clear. However, I foresee coming back to this chapter some time in the future so as to clear out some of the ludicrous words: like 'miscegenations' and 'nemophiliac' above and even the vexed phrase 'unvexing the texture of text' itself. There is a much better way to communicate—and that's pithily. Succinctly. Simply simply.

Also we have the passages of purple prose themselves. I need to return and use all my simplification skills.

Take for example the following paragraph:

G told Suzie he wanted to be a ringmaster, after all. Suzie—in some bemused response more fitting for a 'Big Brother' contestant—said G would do well in the Circus of the Tourettes (as it was called) and she would tease out support for him when approaching the caravan or medicine-wagon where such employment decisions were made. Diary-rooms were not always purpose-built, you see. Dairy-rooms, likewise, as the bovine racers slowed to a near-halt towards the border between reality and fiction.

That whole chapter is abominable, not just that single paragraph. I will now return to change the above paragraph to:

G—who needed a job after leaving hospital—told Suzie about some laughable ambitions of becoming a celebrity on TV. He would drink more milk to help keep his bones strong and his teeth white for smiling. And she would go with him regularly to the local Job Centre Plus as moral support. There, they made him keep a job-seeking diary. It's a joy, not a job, they said.

Not too bad. Needs more work, perhaps, before I make the final alteration. Revision and exegesis are hard taskmasters.

That last bit needs to go. Exegesis? It just popped out before I could self-censor it. Hmm. My head is slowly vanishing at the thought of this whole chapter being edited out during any future publication process. Without the words I simply cannot exist.

Even if I do disappear through retrospective editing, I shall feel it a job worth doing. Indeed, a joy. As a result of all our work (including my own work as a simplon that may vanish before you have the chance to see it) there *will* be a new majestic Festival for Glastonbury that should even rival Wagner's Bayreuth. Perhaps I'm the sad ghost of Thomas Hardy. But no room for doubters.

∞

In the same way as a character becomes thinner without words, when a novella doesn't have enough words it becomes a short story. And if you suck out most or all of the words—as the monster Simplon threatens to do—then you have only a story left, or even a prose poem or vignette, followed ineluctably by the blinding blankness of an empty page. I doubt whether the last paragraph of the previous chapter were Simplon's words at all. They seem too sincere. Too optimistic. Too deft.

I now need to pre-empt his cynical methods of by-passing the Narrative Hospital by saving this work at least as a novella. I sadly need to cauterise it. Preserve it at its current length and consistency.

The circus finally left its pitch near Wells Cathedral and travelled England's new deserts along the banks of the dried-out yellow river towards Glistenberry—if only for old time's sake. The Weirdmonger wished to sell his remaining desiccations of rudery at a makeshift Wagger Market. Just one more Death's throe before the final curtain.

The Torless hill was no longer a Magic Mountain. The Weirdmonger wondered if perhaps the whole Earth itself was the Magic Mountain with a trick or two left up its volcanic sleeve to perform at the greatest Festival of all. Wishful thinking. Or perhaps just another Death in Venice. Or Suicide in Samarkand.

Yet it was a glorious day. The sun stood still, it seemed. And thousands built a massive stage near the ruined Ruins of Glistenberry Abbey. No longer a need for a tent like the Big Top. The whole world could today look and listen, with no entry fee at all. No cost to read about it. Just, hopefully, a magnificent panoply or art and entertainment.

Rutland Boughton's opera *The Immortal Hour* was performed with flair and majesty. Followed by the guest appearance from the realms of reality itself by that fine group Goldwrap. Finally a recitation of Proustian prose to the backdrop of chamber music by Saint-Saens. And four girls called the Supremes—a name borrowed from reality. Their smiles were broad. Their youth rediscovered without having to grow old first.

The Weirdmonger proudly acted as Master of Ceremonies, wrapped in nothing but bronzed and tattooed skin. He'd forgotten his wild youth when the words on his skin had been ruder. Today they were mellifluous and meaningful. Body-words newly branded by the fire of passion in his loins.

Then it became more of a circus again, rather than a music concert. First a clown with red rosettes who made origami models of sea-vessels with newspapers and sculptures from balloons and dreams from ring-cycles of smoke. He even tricked the audience into believing it was real magic.

Then the etched 'writing' of snail trails and trapeze acrobatics against the bluest sky imaginable, beating any wash-day into a cocked hat.

And, with a brassy flourish, Mary of Mangle strode from one side of the stage, Captain Bintiff from the other. Hugely tall figures that seemed to walk on stilts without the necessity of stilts. They mock-fought for the possession of the Weirdtongue. Cut and thrust. With stage blood. Until both of them shared their fleshy plunder with the silence of an eternal deep-throated kiss.

As an echo of Shakespearean power as well as a quaintly miniaturised mirroring of the kiss they had just witnessed on the stage, our two main protagonists, Gregory and Suzie, emerged from air-raid shelters to share their own long (if not eternal) kiss. Only ceasing to catch their breaths. Their names or lineage now irrelevant to their love.

As a coda to the performance—a perhaps more serious moment by which the New Glistenberry Festival would be most remembered—there bloomed, in increasing stridency, Penderecki's 'Threnody for Stringed Instruments', while six million bony human creatures emerged from the ground, smoked from their lairs into freedom, ready to clamber, like stick-insects, over the hopefully *soon-to-be-grassed-over-grazed-over-again* fields of the Summerset Zodiac.

The paradise garden is a magical place. We can only dream when there, but we cannot dream of it.

We shall never know whether the Weirdmonger recognised the clown with red rosettes. Because, as dusk swells within our vision like fairy gold, we must head back towards our own reality, along with Goldwrap.

'Gout cat! Spout cat! Watch their whiskers sprout, cat!'—a costermonger's cry gently echoed as it silted into the horizon of the wonderful place we'd just left. Never to return.

He had left no scraps. In fact, he had no scraps to leave.

The King in Yellow - A Spectral Tragedy
Raymond Lefebvre
October 2005 – 978-0-9551829-0-7

The Just Maybe… Stories
James Scott
July 2006 – 978-0-9551829-1-4

Bookworms I
Some Strange Experiences in Cheltenham
D. P. Woveweft
November 2006 – 978-0-9551829-3-8

Darker Later
James Scott
August 2007 – 978-0-9551829-9-0

Green and Unpleasant Land
The InkerMen
November 2007 – 978-0-9556259-0-9

Lands End
The InkerMen
August 2008 — 978-0-9556259-3-0

Loss
The InkerMen
September 2009 — 978-0-9556259-9-2

Cold Turkey
The InkerMen
December 2009 — 978-0-9556259-5-4

Pieces for Puppets and Other Cadavers
D. P. Watt
August 2010 (2nd Edition) – 978-0-9562749-3-9